# VIRUS WARS

*I would like to dedicate this book to mom and dad. You always supported me no matter what I faced in life and helped mold me into the man I've become.*

*To my sister Misty for putting up with me through our childhood. I couldn't have had a better sister.*

*To my kids. You always keep life interesting and provide so much joy in my life.*

*To Heidi. You are always an encouragement to me. One day we will make it to that tropical beach. 1 4 3.*

*To Matt Hanson for the wicked cool cover art.*

*Finally, I would like to thank God for this opportunity and for his endless grace. May your name be glorified, and your spirit guide our lives.*

# VIRUS WARS

## THE BEGINNING OF THE END

Advantage
BOOKS

# DREW MALLERY

**Library of Congress Catalog Number:** 2022937187

| | |
|---|---|
| **Names:** | Mallery, Drew, Author |
| **Title:** | *The Virus Wars: The beginning of the end* / Drew Mallery |
| **Publisher** | Advantage Books, 2022 |
| **Identifiers:** | ISBN (print): 9781597556934 |
| | (mobi, epub): 9781597557023 |
| **Subjects:** | Fiction: General |

First Printing June 2022
22 23 24 25 26 27   10 9 8 7 6 5 4 3 2 1

# Table of Contents

*Drew Mallery*

# Prologue

After the virus years, the whole world changed. No one really knows how many people lost their lives over those years but we do know that entire villages, towns, cities, and even countries, were left without one survivor.

There was no one to run factories or plants that could produce electricity. So it only took a few months and most communication was cut off around the world. Most people were left to scavenge for food and supplies. In the colder countries, the first few winters were very difficult. People would seek shelter wherever they could and find anything they could to burn for heat.

It was within those first few years that world leaders came up with a radical plan. They would form one central government that would oversee food supplies, shelter and trade. Each country would have a representative that would be housed in the capital of their country. They quickly realized that with so few people living in their countries, it became difficult to supply survivors with basic needs, so they formed a solution.

At first the solution sounded good, and it was for our protection. It soon began to look like something different. The world government began to move everyone from their homes and move them into the capital of their country. Each capital had an airport so there could still be world travel and trade. The cities were surrounded with windmills and solar panels to provide power for the city. Factories were opened and business were profitable again. It looked like the world had picked up the pieces from a great devastation. There was internet again, electric cars to limit pollution and even movie theatres.

With great populations of people, crime was soon to follow. The government created a world wide gun ban. Every gun on the earth was destroyed except for those that the police used to keep order. The world police were feared by the people. There was zero tolerance for crime. When the enforcement officers came to take the criminal, no one knows where they really went. Some people believe that there is a world prison in the northern territory of what used to be Canada. What ever the government was doing with the criminals seemed to be working. This approach from the government resulted in next to no crime.

There was still constant fear of the virus returning. Once again the world government came up with a solution. They fit everyone with a microchip in their right hand. This chip monitored every citizens location (which could also be used for law enforcement), but we were told that the main purpose was to monitor our location in case there was an outbreak of the virus. The chip also monitored each citizens temperature, blood sugars, and other important vital signs. It was so accurate that enforcement officers would show up to your home to force quarantine before you even knew you were sick. Too many people it felt like things were going back to normal like the nightmare had ended. A new world was beginning to take shape. There were, however, many people who felt like this was not a step into a dream world but rather it was a step into an even worse nightmare.

At first the government allowed people to live outside of the city walls, but they soon claimed that those living outside of the city may be carriers of the virus. They claimed that those who were not in favour of this new world order were a threat to the existence of the human race. As a result, they gave those outside of the walls 6 months to comply and move into the cities. The outsiders were informed that they would receive their chip and be given a profession when they moved into the Capital. After the six months grace period, the government began to round up those who the government identified as rebels. The rebels were viewed as criminals and were treated as such.

The enforcement officers would enter a town, long since abandoned, and search for the rebels. If there were any rebels found, they were quickly round up and shipped away. If a rebel resisted, they were met with force and without mercy. Those living in these abandoned towns knew the familiar sound of the searcher drones that constantly patrolled the land, so we would run and hide anywhere we could.

Life outside of the Capital was difficult. There was no electricity and the people lived off the land and hunted for survival. Although most towns were completely abandoned and grown over with trees, it was still home to many forgotten families. To a Rebel, home and family was the most important thing in life, besides God.

The rebels had a contentment even in the difficult circumstances life offered. There was a moral code to love your neighbour. We never saw other survivors as the enemy but rather friends. When ever we saw a rebel enter our town, we would always invite them to our shelter. We would offer the strangers what food we had and shelter for the night.

Most rebels were praying folks. We turned to God when the world seemed like it was ending. This meant that most rebels had something in common the moment we met. No one had much and we struggled to survive. Our lives were filled with love, faith, and peace, even in these difficult times. As difficult as things seemed to this point, nothing could prepare our family for what was about to come next.

# 1

# How It All Began

The sun was just coming out and the birds were starting to chirp outside the window. Zavier knew that this was his cue. He hated doing his chores. He didn't understand why he needed to be the one to go down to the river every morning to get the water. Surly one of his brothers or even his sister could do it. At least once in a while. But nope, it always had to be him.

Zavier drug himself slowly out of bed and took one last look at his siblings, just to make sure none of them were going to jump up and offer to go for him. But alas, he was not so lucky and began to make his way to the river.

The walk was not very long and Zavier could almost see it from where the family was taking shelter. The family decided to take shelter in the old Sussex Corner School. It had been long since abandoned when the government moved everyone to the Capital. His dad said that it was a perfect place to take shelter because there were many exits, with lots of rooms to hide in if the enforcement officers made a sweep through the now abandoned town.

Zavier could remember the pre virus years well, when the town was always full of people and when the biggest care of life was if he was going to get a new brawler in his favourite video game. But now things were very different. There were only a few families left in the town but no one ever tells each other where we live, just in case the officers find a family and torture them to tell them where other families live. The town is grown over with trees and bushes now but some places are still familiar, like the old McDonalds and Tim Hortons. The family never really goes that far into town anymore, or ventures very far from our shelter. The river seems to be the farthest we venture out and sometimes the kids will sneak over to their old house in the trailer park. Their parents were never too happy when they did. They always said that it was the first place officers would go look. Zavier wondered if any of the family was even out of bed yet, as he could see the river just ahead of him.

Zaiden could hear Zavier get up, like every morning. Every morning was the same. He knew when Zavier was awake because he would hear him sigh, drag himself out of bed, then he would begin to walk out the door. He would always pause at the doorway for some reason, he was meaning to ask him why some day, then he would exit and we wouldn't see him for the next hour or so.

When Zavier left, Zaiden knew it was his turn to get up. He had his chores to do but he really didn't mind his chores. His job was to gather the food from the garden and search the bushes for berries. He was the family scavenger. It was Zaiden who would find the cool things. One time, he went into one of the houses down the road from their shelter and he found an old cell phone in a bedside table. The really cool thing was that it still had some battery life left in it. He brought it home to the family and they watched some of the old videos that the previous owner had made. For the next few days, the family was sharing memories of when there were cars, electricity and fast food. Man he missed his fast food and bagels. His mouth was beginning to water just thinking about what he remembered bagels tasting like.

When the government moved everyone to the city, they shut off all electricity in rural areas. The government wanted to have everyone living in the same city, and they figured the best way to accomplish this was to take away all the luxuries they knew. It worked. Most people willingly moved from their homes and families, to have all the things we enjoyed. One time a man came through the town and said that he heard that in the city they still have tv, internet, fast food, and even bagels. Man what he wouldn't give for a bagel.

As Zadien got up and made his way out of the room, he went to the old cafeteria in the school. It had enough windows that they were able to grow some plants inside. He always loved to grow plants, and who would have known that it would one day help feed his family. He planted melons, berries and even an avocado tree. The tree actually grew nicely. His mom and him built a wooden box and put soil in it a few years ago. They planted potatoes, carrots, cucumbers and just about anything they could fit in it. Truthfully, he didn't really like any of it but his mom and dad always told him he needed to eat it if he was going to be healthy. The honest truth is that he wished he could grow bagels. That would be sweet.

As Zaiden began to pick some of their berries and get some of the food from the garden, he heard a noise behind him. As he turned he could see Ezra and his dad walking out the door. They always got up early to go to the river to fish, and if they saw any animals along the way, it would mean an extra meal for the family.

Ezra could hear his dad coming down the hall long before he ever got there. He could hear him humming a song, he is always humming and singing something. He always told the kids, "it's not about the circumstances we face, it's how we face the circumstance." He and mom were always trying to find ways to make life a little more enjoyable. It didn't seem like any song or any game could change the fact that he missed his old life from time to time. He remembered when he played hockey every winter and he got to travel from town to town and play. Ezra heard from a traveler one time, that they still play hockey in the cities. Once a year, the Capital takes its' best team and they travel to another Capital in another country. They play other teams, from other countries, and the best part of all is that they have TV's and can watch the games. It sounded just like what we used to do.

As his dad approached, he knew that it was time to get up and get to the river. He grabbed his fishing pole and his bow and arrow. The family had went into town after the first Gathering and found some bows and arrows in the old Canadian Tire. Since then, the family practiced everyday. His mom and dad told the kids the importance of being able to survive if anything ever happened to them.

Ezra and dad made their way out of the old school and begin to make their way to their fishing hole. Since no one really lived around here anymore, nature pretty much took over. There was always deer, birds and every other animal wandering around. The brooks and streams were full of fish. If you couldn't catch a fish in the brook, you really were not trying. You could reach in and pick them up with your hands if you really wanted to.

As they were leaving the school, he could hear his mom yelling from the doorway.

"Good luck boys! have fun!"

As he turned to look, he could see his dad blowing her a kiss, but being a bit goofy while he did it. He always acted a little goofy. Zavier always says that we have a weird dad. Behind his mom, Ezra could see Azalia making her way out as well.

If there was one thing that Azalia hated more than anything, it was having to get up. What she wouldn't give to just have a day where she could sleep in and not have to get up. She could remember when life was so much easier than this. She loved talking with friends and listening to her BTS albums. Man she would love to hear just one song from them again. It's been years since she saw even a picture of them, but just thinking of them warmed her heart. She wondered to herself where they were and what they were doing right now. As quick as the thought came into her mind, she was snapped back into the real world by the sound of her mom's voice.

"Azalia?"

"What mom!" Azalia was still in a daze and half asleep but she knew what was coming next.

"The boys are all gone, and we need to get breakfast started before they get back."

Her mom's voice was one of slight panic. She knew that her mom liked to have the food ready for when the boys got home. Azalia hopped out of bed and made her way into the cafeteria. As she was walking in, she could see Ezra snd Drew walking across the field towards the water. She knew they had a little time to get everything done before the boys returned. Besides, she didn't see the water they needed and she figured that Zavier should be back by now. She thought to herself that he must have got distracted with something.

She remembered the time Zavier came home with an old guitar he found in one of the homes near by, but had failed to bring the water that he was suppose to get. The kids found it funny but mom and Drew didn't find it quite as amusing. But to Zavier's credit, we still play that guitar today. Drew is no BTS, but… well, let's just say that he is no BTS.

As Azalia and her mom made their way down the long halls of the school, you could hear the sounds of the chickens, and smell them, long before you got to the room. They had to have the chickens inside because if there was any sign of life, when the government drones fly over, the enforcement officers would arrive within the day. The family could hear the familiar humming sound of the drones a couple times a week. Sometimes they would hear them late at night, but sometimes the drones would fly by in the middle of the day. The family would have to take shelter whenever they heard the sound of the oncoming drones. Every time they came, it was always the same routine. Their hearts would beat so hard that it felt like it was coming out of their chest, and this time would be no different.

Everyone was going about their chores, like every morning, when the deafening hum of what sounded like hundreds of drones began to be heard overhead. Azalia and Heidi took one quick look at one another, and as if they shared the same mind, whispered, "The Boys!"

# 2

# The Arrival

"Man I hate getting the water! Why couldn't someone else be the one to go get the water?"

The thought barely left Zavier's mind when he heard the sound of the drones.

Something was different about the sound this time. It took a few moments to identify the new sound but it hit him like ton of bricks. It was the hum of the governments vehicles as well. Electric vehicles have a very distinct hum. This was the first time the enforcement officers were sent with drones. Zavier figured that this must mean that the government was not messing around.

Zavier peeked through the bushes by the stream to see if he could see anything over head. It was like the sky had turned black. There were so many drones that it seemed to block out the sun. He could see a vehicle on what used to be the main street though town. The government vehicles were all headed in the same direction. Right toward the school.

Ezra and dad were getting their fishing gear together when they heard the sound of the drones.

"Mom, Azalia, and Zaiden are still in the school!" "Do you think they hear them?" The panic in Ezra's voice did not escape Drew's notice.

"They will be ok! We have gone over the escape plans and exercises many times before."

Drew was trying to reassure Ezra, but he wasn't even sure he believed what he said. They had heard the drones many times before but never so many, and never accompanied by the enforcement officers. Something was different this time. He wondered if they had not been careful enough and been spotted by a drone somehow?

As the pair slowly made their way from the fishing hole, they stopped at the edge of the tree line. They peered across the field to see what was happening. What the two saw sent fear so deep that it felt like it was shaking their bones. The entire sky was filled with drones. What they saw on the ground truly sent shivers up their spine.

Parked in front of the school were 10 trucks each filled with 10 enforcement officers. The officers had all gotten out of their vehicles and seemed to be just chatting and taking a break. It was obvious that the group was passing through and Sussex wasn't their target. There was a Gathering about to take place but it wasn't going to be Sussex this time. There were rumours from some travellers that a settlement had started near, what used to be called, St.Martins. Drew wondered out loud to Ezra if that was where the Government was going.

From the corner of his eye, Ezra saw movement. He knew that the watering hole was in that direction and that Zaiver would be there now. He just hoped that Zavier would stay put, but as fate would have it, he was not that lucky. He could see Zavier at the edge of the tree line and he could tell that he was thinking of making a run for the school. Ezra began to pray that Zavier would just stay put. The boy knew how to fight but there was just too many people. Even for someone who had been training as much as their family.

The family had found shelter in the old library after the first Gathering. One day dad had found a training book for muay thai. He was convinced that the family needed to train and learn how to fight just in case the government arrived one day. If there is one thing everyone knows about dad, it's that he is always prepared. So for the last few years they had spent a couple hours a day training. Dad aways said that there was going to be a day that we were happy he was so hard on us to learn as much as we could. Truth be told, the boys really liked it. It was their favourite part of the day. Azalia would rather do anything else besides train. Her effort was, as one might put it, lacking. Here they were now, and Ezra wondered if all the training was going to have to be put to use.

Heidi and Azalia had quickly retreated to the cafeteria the moment they heard the sound of the drones. Rule one in their escape plan was to make sure no one got left behind, and Azalia knew that Zaiden must be in that direction somewhere. Azalia was growing tired of always running and trying to hide. She was tired of trying to work so hard for their food and living like it was the 1800's. What she wouldn't give to just be able to sit down on a computer and chat again. Just one last time. Azalia wanted to listen to her Favourite band. She wanted to head the familiar voices of BTS, just one more time.

Azalia's mom and Zaiden had already filled a back pack each and thrown it over their backs. Rule number two was to gather food on the way out. They were making their way to the rear exit of the building. This was why the school was the perfect shelter. That's what Drew used to say. There were so many exits that if the enforcement officers came in one door, they could slip out another door. They could be long gone before the officers realized that there was someone living in the school.

As they made their way to the exit, her mom stopped. Azalia could tell by the posture that her mom was worried. As her mom turned, the look in her eyes confirmed it, something was very wrong.

As Heidi grabbed both of her kids, the only thought in her mind was how she was going to protect her children. She had practiced this drill a hundred times. The family would go out of this exit and make their way across the field of high grass. Once across the grass they would make their way into the tree line. From there they would get to the water where they would not be easily tracked. This was rule number three. Make sure that you can not be followed. But this plan did not allow for the over abundance of drones or the hundred guards standing around the building.

As the three approached the exit, Heidi could see the shadow of an enforcement officer. The three family members snuck behind an old desk that was laying on its' side. From this vantage point they watched the door. They could see the officer wiping the dust and dirt off the window and began to peer inside. As long as they don't move, they thought that the officer should leave. Heidi thought that they should be fine and this will just be another story to tell the travellers as they come through. She knew that this hope was the only thing keeping her from going crazy with fear.

Zaiden was sure he could hear his mom's heart beating through her chest, This was bad. They had never seen so many officers and certainly not that many drones. He could hear a couple officers chatting through the door. They were saying that they had to be to the St.Martins settlement before night and they were going to need to leave soon. The officers were saying that they would have to leave soon if they were going to make it. Zaiden knew that if they could just remain quiet for a few minutes that the officers would leave and everything would be fine.

"Did you see that?"

The officer sounded like something had just caught his attention and the thought sent Zaiden's mind racing,

"Had they seen us? We haven't moved, and we were so careful. How could they have seen us?" Zaiden was whispering to his mom. He was about to make a run for it when he felt his mom's hand on his shoulder. Her finger was to her lips and was signalling him to remain quiet.

"I think I just saw something move at the tree line." The way the officer spoke made it sound like he was quite convinced.

Zaiden could only think of the boys outside of the school. Surly they would have remained in the woods and were not going to try and come back on a rescue mission... right?

"We have movement on the tree line."

Zaiden could see the officer talking into his sleeve. He figured that he must be talking to someone on a radio. The officer had obviously seen something, but maybe it was just an animal? Zaiden's mind was starting to run away on him as he began to wonder how they were going to react if the family was spotted. Would they fight? Would they run? Would they get caught? Would they be killed or captured? The thoughts running through his head were becoming so loud it was deafening. He had to calm his mind down. Zaiden began to pray.

"We will send a few guys over. You guys check it out, and the rest of us are going to head out."

The voice on the other end of the radio was obviously the man in charge. "You need a drone left with you?" The voice sounded almost irritated.

"We should be ok, we will only be a minute, and we will catch up."

Zaiden knew that it had to be one of the boys. He hoped that it was just an animal, but something inside told him that this was not going to turn out well.

Zavier watched as the drones started to move in a way that looked like waves in the ocean. They moved all together in the same direction. Then as one would change direction, they would all move in unison and follow. The vehicles started to fill with the soldiers and they started to move out. All except one truck. Zavier had lifted his head to get a good look over the tall grass that stood between him and the school. When he did, one of the soldiers was looking right in his direction. He hoped that he hadn't been spotted, but he could see the soldier talking in his sleeve. Now there were five soldiers walking strait towards him. Zavier just knew that this was not going to be good.

Zavier thought to himself that if he could just stay low and wait long enough, the drones and the other trucks will just leave. He thought that it will only be about ten soldiers against the family, and Zavier liked those odds.

Drew and Ezra could see the soldiers moving in the direction of Zavier and knew this was only going to end one way. They were going to need to take these soldiers out, and fast. If the soldiers had time to radio ahead to the others then there was going to be too many soldiers. Between the drones and the soldiers, there was not going to be an escape.

"Ezra," Drew whispered. "Get your bow ready. We are only going to get one shot at this. If those soldiers radio the others, it's all over. We are going to need to be fast, and then we need to get the girls and Zaiden and get out of this area."

Ezra was hearing his dad loud and clear. He knew that if he could take one or two of the soldiers down fast enough that his dad and Zavier could attack the remaining soldiers. The fight would be over before the soldiers even knew they were in a fight.

Drew and Ezra began to slowly make their way through the tall grass. They stayed as low as possible in an effort not to be seen. As they approached the soldiers, they were now close enough to hear the grass swiping against the soldier's uniforms. With one last look at his father, Ezra drew back his bow and stood. He had revealed himself in the tall grass. There was no turning back.

# 3

# Taken

The moment that Zavier saw Ezra stand he knew that it was now or never. Ezra got two shots off so quickly that the second soldier had an arrow through him before his comrade even hit the ground. As if it had been planned for days, the second soldier was being hit as Zavier saw his dad emerge from the tall grass. He looked like a lion pouncing on its' prey. Drew soared through the air, seemingly to defy gravity, plunging both knees into the third soldier. The force of the impact drove the soldier to the ground.

Zavier was only a couple feet away when he saw a fourth soldier lifting his pulse gun toward Ezra. In one swift motion, Zavier pushed the barrel of the gun into the air as the shot fired from the gun. The sound was deafening in his ears. He punched the soldier's elbow downward and followed through with his own elbow. The maneuver resulted in Zavier's elbow being planted into the temple of the soldier. The soldier was out cold before he touched the ground.

Ezra saw the punch coming at the last moment. The fifth soldier had made a move toward him the moment he stood in the grass. Ezra knew he was coming and he lifted his arm to block the attack. As the soldier's fist connected with his arm, Ezra crouched down, twirled around and swept the soldier's feet from underneath him. Ezra could hear the soldier grunt as he landed on the ground with a thump. Ezra was on top of him before he even knew what happened. Standing above the soldier, and with the most heroic voice he could muster, Ezra exclaimed, "You picked the wrong place for a rest." With one quick punch the soldier was out.

Heidi knew that the soldiers must be getting close to Zavier. She was hoping that he had hidden himself well enough. The thought barely escaped her mind when she saw Ezra stand up, not five feet from the soldiers. Ezra had his bow drawn. In an instant she knew that she had to distract the soldiers at the door so they wouldn't call for reinforcements.

"Hey you!! You looking for us?"

Before Heidi could formulate a plan, she heard Azalia's voice call out to the soldiers a few feet away.

Azalia had watched as her brothers and Drew were subduing the soldiers in the field, and before she could think of what to do next, she heard her own voice shouting at the soldiers at the door. She wondered if maybe that wasn't the best idea until she saw Zaiden soaring through the air.

Zaiden saw the other boys stand and knew instantly what must be done. He could hear his sister shouting as he was lunging at the door. As if it was perfectly planned, it distracted the soldiers at the door long enough that they did not see the strike coming. Zaiden surprised the first soldier as he mashed through the door. Zaiden was able to lay a blow to his chest and knock the wind out of him before he even knew that Zaiden was there. The other soldier swung his fist at Zaiden but he ducked the attack. Using the second soldier as a shield, Zaiden pushed him towards the first. Not before he got a shot off with the pulse gun. The second soldier wouldn't have felt a thing as the pulse from the gun collided with his chest. He was on the ground the moment the blast hit him.

The soldier got the first shot off but that would be the only shot fired. Before the second shot went off, Heidi had kicked the side of the soldier's leg so hard that it almost broke it in half. Zaiden laid a firmly planted knee into the soldier's chin as the he was dropping. Both soldiers laid on the ground motionless.

Zaiden and his mom could hear what sounded like a truck door closing and the familiar hum of the vehicle as it pulled away. This was bad. They knew that they were going to need to pack up and get out before the reinforcements arrived. They managed to fend off a few soldiers, but over a hundred was quite another thing. It was in that moment that Heidi noticed that Azalia was not with them. Where was Azalia?

Azalia remembered shouting and seeing Zaiden smash through the door. It was in that moment that there was a searing pain and her whole world went black. Azalia could hear a steady hum in her ear as she was gaining consciences. There was something else though. Something that she never thought she would ever hear again. She could hear the sound of music. It had been so long since she had heard music. Oh how she had missed that sound.

She could feel her body shaking back and forth and she knew that she was moving. She began to become aware that there was something holding her in place as she attempted to move. She opened her eyes and realized that she was strapped to the floor of a vehicle. This was not how she imagined her first car ride in years.

# 4

# A Whole New World

It had been a long time since Azalia had been in a vehicle. It had been equally as long since she had heard music playing on a radio. She knew that she should be afraid that she had been taken captive, but there was a sense of excitement at experiencing what being a normal person felt like.

She found herself being lost in her memories for a moment. The memories of going for family drives. The memories of turning on her Alexa and listening to music for hours. She found herself thinking about what it was like to drive through a McDonalds drive through. These were all things that she hadn't experienced in years.

She was thinking about the movies she had watched in the theatres and times she chatted with friends on the internet. She was thinking about these distant memories when she was suddenly blindsided by the memory of the Gathering. It was the last day that she had a normal life. She remembered that there was a broadcast running on the tv and radio all day.

"This is Prime Minister Treadon. It was announced months ago that this day was coming and it has finally arrived."

Azalia can remember seeing Drew cringe every time he heard Treadon's voice.

"For your safety, we have gathered our people into the Capital. The virus could return in any moment for another wave. We have made a choice for the people, to protect you all. We can not get through this without each other. We all must do our part. We must all ensure that we are safe through our efforts. We are aware that there are those who do no want to comply and they are leaving us all at risk. We will begin a program to gather those who fail to comply. Starting tomorrow we will bring them to the Capital. Here they will be given a final choice to do their part to protect the people or they will be removed for being a threat to the well being of us all."

Azalia can remember seeing her mom and Drew getting more and more uneasy as the day went on. The public announcement ended with a final ominous statement from Treadon.

"At midnight tonight all power will be diverted to the city. Those who chose life will live life to the fullest. Those who chose death will not drag us down. You will be removed and forgotten."

She could remember that statement well, because until now, it was the last thing she had ever heard on a radio. The government had given us six months to move to the Capital. Time had run out.

Mom and Drew had heard enough that day. They took us to a familiar hiking spot. The locals called the trail the Bluff and it had a reputation for being quite beautiful. It was a cliff that overlooked the valley and was so peaceful. As beautiful as the sight was, it couldn't keep our minds away from the fear being propagated on the radio.

Those living in the town were not scared the first time we heard the loud hum of an army of drones. We were curious. People went outside of their shelters to see what was going on. The drones filled the skies. They simply paused for a moment then moved on. The enforcement officers entered the town less than a day later. It was the first time we saw the officers but it wouldn't be the last. They didn't ask questions. They didn't hesitate. They wouldn't stop.

They started to fire their guns and people were running for their lives. There were too many officers to resist. Everyone in town found anywhere they could to hide but the officers were relentless. They continued to look for anyone hiding. This lasted for days. Our family was on the bluff when the drones first flew over head and Drew and Mom were insistent that we could not come off the mountain yet. For the next few days we could hear the sounds of screaming and gun fire coming from the valley. We spent almost a week on that cliff.

We couldn't hear any noise, or see any lights in the night, for a few days before we ventured back into town. When we arrived there was no one there. The drones were gone. The officers were gone. The people were gone.

"Hey! Are you listening? Do you want some chocolate or not?"

Azalia had snapped back from her memories to reality. She realized that the officer was talking to her.

"Do you want a piece of chocolate? Last offer."

The officer didn't sound angry at all. He didn't sound much like what she thought they would. I guess she thought they would sound almost evil. The reality was that he sounded very much human. Almost compassionate.

Azalia had not had a piece of chocolate in years so she nodded that she would like some. The officer gently unstrapped her constraints and let her sit up on the floor of the vehicle.

"You know that we are not here to hurt you right? We are here to help."

Azalia barely registered that he even spoke. The taste of something other then meat or veggies was filling her mind with joy. With the food still very much filling her mouth, Azalia retorted.

"The fact that you knocked me over the head and drug me unconsciously into your van says otherwise. Nothing says 'We are just trying to help you,' like knocking someone out and dragging them away." Her comments were dripping with sarcasm but she could tell that the officer was trying to hold back a smirk.

"Listen, if we just asked you politely you would never had come. Besides, how do you think we are going to react to a family of ninjas?"

Azalia could tell he was trying to be funny with his last statement. She found her self trying to hold back a smirk of her own.

"You'll see that the life you are living now is nothing compared to what awaits you in the city."

It was in that moment that Azalia realized what was truly happening. For the first time in her life, her parents were not going to be able to make the decisions for her. This was all on her. This was going to be a choice between life and death and she was only going to have a few days to decide.

She had some mixed emotions over the next day. She missed her family and hoped that they were safe, but she had been talking with the officers and they seemed friendly. They had allowed her to take off the restraints early in the journey. They asked a few questions about life on the "outside," as they called it, but mostly the conversations were light. They let her listen to BTS for a lot of the journey. It was something she had dreamed about for years. She had no way to hear their music since the power went out. She just couldn't shake this uneasy feeling. There still seemed to be a fear in her heart even though the officers seemed friendly enough. She knew that something wasn't right about this.

Azalia could hear the sound of a hum long before she could see what was causing it. She could see windmills as far as the eyes could see as they got closer to the Capital. The hum became deafening as they drove through the endless fields of them. The sound had become so loud that the soldiers didn't speak. They knew that with all the noise you would have to holler to be heard. When they were approaching the windmills, one of the officers started to explain how they powered the Capital with them. The truth is that she tuned the soldier out. She could care less how the Capital was powered.

What Azalia saw next took her breath away. There was a large wall built. It was the largest wall she had ever seen. Behind the wall stood buildings higher than she had ever seen. There were digital billboards on half the buildings that were advertising movies and food. They advertised concerts and what looked like news clips from around the world. It was like nothing she had ever seen before.

Azalia began to notice the people as the large doors opened and the van entered through the gate. There were people from all over the world. They were laughing and joking. It looked like she had just entered into paradise. It was everything that she longed for and more. There was so much noise. The noise was coming from the sounds of passing cars, the voices of people and even the sounds from the adds playing on the buildings.

Azalia was glued to the window as they made their way through the Capital. She could tell that the soldiers were slightly entertained by her excitement but she didn't care. This was simply amazing.

They drove by an airport and Azalia could see an airplane coming in for a landing. She continued to watch the runway and another plane sped down the runway for takeoff. She was trying to keep her eyes on the plane when the van came to a stop.

"This is where we hand you off."

Azalia looked out the front of the van and saw a heavily fortified wall. There was another van waiting for them on the other side. She heard a voice in one of the officer's radio announce the transfer of the rebel was complete as she was transferred from one van to the next. She knew that it was her they were referring to but she didn't feel much like a rebel. She kind of liked this place.

The new guards never spoke a word to her. It was a ride of complete silence except for the hum of the vehicle. The ride was short and ended at the doors of a large stone building. She was taken from the van and brought inside where she was placed in a large empty room. The room was decorated with flags, some pictures of world leaders (She remembered them from when they still had TV.), and various arial views of the Capital. She was taken back by its' size and beauty.

"Welcome to my home."

The voice came from behind Azalia but it was one that she recognized from the radio. It was the last voice she had ever heard from a radio and was a voice that she would never forget. She saw the man standing in the doorway when she turned to look at where the voice was coming from. She knew exactly who she was looking at. Prime Minister Treadon.

"Do not be afraid of me. I have no desire to hurt you. I only want to help make your life so much better."

She noticed that Treadon always talked with a smile. He even smiled when nothing was said to smile about. She did not trust this guy.

"I know that you must have a ton of questions but let's get you fed. We will bring you some nice clothes. I will gladly answer anything you want to know."

Azalia had a lot of questions, but the first one on her mind was where her family was. She wasn't sure that she could believe anything Treadon said but she didn't see any harm in getting some good food and nice clothes. What could possibly go wrong with that?

# 5

# The Gifting

Ezra kept playing the scene over in his mind. He thought to himself that there must have been something he could have done. He remember that moment well. He was standing over the body of the soldier when he could see another soldier carrying Azalia off to the van. The soldier threw the body into the back and the van sped off. It all happened so fast and he simply froze in place. He wanted to yell but he couldn't make a sound. He wanted to run but he was frozen in place. As hard as it was to remember not being able to help his sister, what haunted him most was the look on Zavier and Drew's face. They both stood motionless with the same horrified and defeated look, as they watched the van speed away. He could see his mom and Zaiden standing over their defeated foes, but it seemed like neither of them realized Azalia had been taken.

Heidi had heard the door close and heard the van speed off. Her immediate thought was how the family was going to get their stuff gathered and get out of the school before the enforcement officers returned. She knew that this was not going to be good. She could see Zaiden looking into the door of the school and heard him calling for Azalia.

"Hey Azalia! It's safe to come out now. You missed the good stuff. You should have seen how awesome I did!"

Zaiden was still pretty pumped from the fight. He had trained for a couple years but he had never had to use the skills. It felt amazing. He was still on his way into the school when he realized that something didn't seem right. Azalia wasn't answering and there was no movement in the school to be heard. In that moment he realized that Azalia was gone. He could see his mom standing in the doorway as he looked in her direction. By the look on her face, and the tears in her eyes, he knew that she had come to the same realization.

The rest of the day had a strange feeling to it. The family was trying to gather their things, as it became apparent that they needed to find a new shelter now. It was just a matter of time before the enforcement officers returned and they were not going to be able to fight them all. No one spoke most of the day, that was until Drew broke the silence.

"Ok guys, here is the thing. We will not be able to help Azalia if we are just standing around feeling defeated. We have to pull ourselves together and figure out what we are going to do."

Drew was trying to rally the troops but he was met with immediate opposition to the encouragement.

"We can't do anything." Zavier was visibly upset.

"What are we going to do? It's not like we can walk to the Capital, march through the font door, and demand they give us our sister. That is *if* she is even alive!!" Zavier's voice was beginning to raise.

"She is fine!" Zaiden was not even going to entertain the thought that Azalia may be gone forever.

"We need to figure out how we are going to get her back." Zaiden didn't have any sort of plan but he knew that they could not just sit here and do nothing.

"Doesn't the Bible teach us to pray when we don't know what to do?" Ezra was well aware that the family knew what the Bible taught, but he was just trying to get the tension out of the room. He hated to hear the family fight and this was certainly not the time to fight.

"All right then, it's settled. We will take a minute and just pray for some guidance."

The family prayed for much longer than what they were expecting. They prayed for strength in the coming days. They prayed for guidance and direction for the plans that must be laid. They asked for wisdom and encouragement. They asked God to empower them to save their sister, and deliver the world from this evil that seemed to engulf it. The family didn't know it yet, but this prayer was going to be the prayer that changed their lives forever. This was a prayer that would change the course of history.

There seemed to be a burden lifted from the family when they had finished praying. There seemed to be a quiet resolve. They were not sure what they were going to do about Azalia but they knew that God had a plan. What came next was something that no one could have guessed.

Drew asked Ezra to go out and get the fishing poles that were left behind, when they fought the officers. As Ezra was making his way to the stream he could see the poles laying just where he had left them. He Couldn't stop thinking about what he could have done differently to have saved his sister. In a moment of anger he swung his fist and connected with the tree beside him. The tree shook. This was not a small tree. It must have been 3 feet in diameter. Ezra didn't immediately notice that the tree shook because he was more preoccupied with the fact that he didn't feel a thing. It was like punching a pillow. He drew close to the tree to see where he had punched it. He saw that there was a large piece missing from where he had just assaulted it.

"Did I just do that?"

Ezra stood in disbelief. Curiosity got the best of him and he swung again. This time there was no mistaking what he saw. His hand sunk about six inches into the flesh of the tree and the entire tree shook.

"What are you doing?"

Zaiden was walking up to Ezra when he saw him swing at the tree. He could have swore that the tree moved when he hit it, but he figured that it was impossible and dismissed the thought. The thought would not be dismissed for long. He saw the section of the tree that was missing as he stepped closer.

"How are you doing that? Let me see you do it again!"

Zaiden was confused by what he was seeing, but it sure was amazing.

Ezra was startled by his brother's voice. He had no idea that he would be coming down to the stream as well. He wanted to punch the tree again to see if this was for real. He wasn't about to punch it just because his brother wanted him too.

"I'll hit it again when I want to hit it."

Ezra wanted so badly to take another swing, but he was going to wait just long enough that his brother knew he wasn't hitting it because he wanted him to.

"Come on Ezra! I saw you do it! Just hit it again so I can see! I don't understand what the big deal is!"

This was not the time to argue with his brother. Zaiden was getting on his nerves. Frustrated, Ezra moved to shove his brother out of the way. He was about to push his brother when it was like Zaiden was standing beside him, instead of in front of him. Ezra could feel Zaiden's foot connecting with his, and before he could steady himself he was laying on the ground.

Zaiden didn't understand why Ezra wouldn't just punch the tree agin. Zaiden could see the look on Ezra's face as Ezra turned toward him. By the look on his face, Ezra had heard enough. Ezra began to move toward him when it was like the whole world slowed down. Zaiden could see the water in the stream moving as if it was almost standing still. He could see the leaves falling so slowly that it defied gravity. But what was stranger was that Ezra was now moving so slowly that Zaiden could see the muscles in his arms tensing and his feet bracing. Zaiden could see the look in his brother's eyes. It became apparent to him that Ezra was trying to shove him. Zaiden just stepped to his side, and gently placed his foot in front of Ezra.

"This will teach him for trying to shove me."

It was in that moment that the world went back to normal speed. Ezra tripped over his foot and plunged to the ground.

"How did you do that?" Ezra was almost sounding as if he was scared.

"It was like you were standing in front of me one moment, then you were beside me the next. What is happening to us?"

Ezra was confused, but at the same time he knew that this was amazing.

"I was wondering the same thing!" Both the brothers recognized Zavier's voice, but they had not been aware that he was with them.

"Ok Zavier, what did you see?"

Zaiden was curious if he and Ezra were imagining this whole thing, but in an instant he knew it was not some illusion. Something was happening and they had to figure out what. He knew that it was not an illusion as he watched Zavier appear out of thin air.

Zavier was bored, so he snuck out of the school and ran down to see what his brothers were doing. He could see the big tree by the stream shake as he was getting closer and he could hear his brothers talking. He could see Ezra try and shove Zaiden as he was approaching but it was like Zaiden moved faster then his eyes could register. It was like he was standing in one place then was just standing in the other place. He wanted to find out what was going on but he thought that they probably won't tell him anyways, so he thought that he would just sneak up and hear for himself. It was then that he knew something weird was going on.

Everything went black and white but he could see his brothers like glowing figures. There were bushes between them but it was like he was seeing the heat from their bodies though the bushes. He could see the same glow coming from what looked like a squirrel in the tree above them and a rabbit on the other side of the stream that was hiding in the bushes. As he walked to his brothers they just ignored him. He hated when they ignored him. When Ezra asked what was going on and he replied, it was like the whole world went normal again.

Ezra thought to himself that Zavier just appeared out of no where and Zaiden was moving faster than anything he had ever seen before. He almost punched through a tree that was three feet deep. Ezra knew that something was happening, but just what was happening was still a mystery. One thing that became very certain to Ezra in that moment was that they may have just been given the ability to save their sister. God had answered their prayers and they were not going to waist this gift.

# 6

# Time to Move

The boy's parents didn't believe anything the boys were telling them at first. It wasn't until Ezra picked up his mom with one hand, while she was sitting in the chair, that the parents knew something was certainly different about their boys. It was hard to argue that something wasn't going on as she peered down from her perch high above his head. Zaiden had the entire mess in the school cleaned almost as fast as their eyes could register. Zavier was standing in front of them, then in a moment he just wasn't there. What ever was going on, the family knew that God was making something very clear. It was time to save their sister.

"OK guys! We need to figure out what we are going to do here."

Drew was already formulating a game plan before the words even escaped his mouth.

"It won't take long for the government to figure out that they are down an entire group of officers. They will be back and I would assume that they are going to be looking pretty hard for us. We need to gather our things and find another shelter. I think that the old civic centre would be a good place to start. There are enough windows that we can start another garden. We would also be high enough on the hill that we would be able to see any officers coming into town long before they get here."

Everything was going a mile a minute in Drew's mind. He knew that they did not have enough time to hesitate. They needed to take action now, before it was too late.

"What about Azalia?"

The sound of Zaiden's voice almost sounded annoyed.

"We can't just let them take her! We need to do something." Zaiden was starting to raise his voice and you could tell that he was far more concerned with getting his sister back, then finding a new place to live.

"Well we are not going to be able to help her, if we are all dead Zaiden!" Zavier was getting a little annoyed. It was becoming clear that the stress of the situation was starting to get to everyone. It was in that moment that a large boom silenced everyone. Ezra stood a little ways away with his arm buried to his elbow in a concrete wall. He spoke quietly, yet firmly, as he slipped his arm back through the hole he just created.

"We will not find shelter or save our sister unless we are working together. God did not give us these gifts to fight one another. He gave us these gifts to fight our common enemy."

"Let's just get our stuff together! We know that we can't stay here."

Their mom was trying to get things moving but also defuse the situation. Nothing irritated Heidi any more than petty arguments. Now was not the time to argue. Now was the time to move.

The family barely had time to start gathering their things when they heard the familiar sound of the drone. This time the feeling was different. They always knew that the drones were looking for random rebels, but this time they knew that they were being hunted.

The sound of vehicles soon followed and the family knew that they were not getting out of this without a fight. The moment had arrived that they feared would come. Now was the moment that they needed to decide if they were going to fight or surrender. The family had always discussed this day and how they would respond. The family decided long ago they would not give in to the enemy.

Ezra kneeled down beside the door. He knew that he was going to leap into action the moment the officers stepped through that door. Every muscle tensed in his body as he prepared for the biggest fight of his life. Suddenly Zaiden was standing right beside him.

"Let's do this."

It was in an instant and the door was open and Zaiden was no longer standing beside him. Apparently Zaiden had a different plan than him.

Zaiden watched as Ezra knelt beside the door. He thought to himself that he was not going to wait for the officers to come in there after the family. He knew that they needed to take the fight to them. Zaiden knew that even with their guns, the officers couldn't hit what they couldn't see. He lunged for the door then stopped beside Ezra.

"Let's do this."

He didn't give Ezra, or his parents, a moment to talk him out of this. He simply opened the door and ran.

The whole world slowed down. It was like the officers were stepping out of their vehicles at a snails pace. As Zaiden reached the first officer he crouched down, swinging his leg around, and swept the officers legs from underneath him. The world went back to normal speed as he watched the officer hit the ground.

"Hey guys! Looks a bit like you came to the wrong spot for a fight."

Zaiden already knew that he could fight. He also knew that the officers didn't stand a chance with this new gift.

The officer right beside him took the first swing. The world slowed again as Zaiden slipped under officer's arm and firmly planted his knee into his chest. The officer crumbled in a heap. Zaiden could see another officer flying through the air from the corner of his eye. He watched as the body collided with the door of another vehicle. He could see another officer bounced off the hood of his parked vehicle and Zaiden knew that he was not alone. Zavier was in the fight.

Zavier was standing at the ready, facing the door. Suddenly the door flew open and Zaiden was gone. Zavier knew that the fight was on. Zavier was out the door before he could even convince himself that this wasn't a good idea. The world went black and white the moment he stepped through the door. He could see the glow of hundreds of bodies. Some standing, and some still sitting in their vehicles.

Zavier could see that Zaiden was taking care of himself, but he noticed an officer raising his gun a few feet away. Zavier punched the officer's elbow downward, and with his other hand he pointed the barrel at the officer. The officer didn't even see what was coming as the stun gun went off. The officer flew threw the air and was out cold before he ever touched the ground.

Another officer stood beside him in disbelief. He was unaware that Zavier was still standing there.

"Peek a Boo!"

Zavier showed himself and the terror in the officers eyes spoke volumes. This was not going to be a long fight and Zavier knew that this victory would be theirs. The world went black and white again as Zavier planted a firm punch to the gut of the officer. Zavier planted a stunning blow to the officer's chin as he bowed over. Zavier leapt over the hood of the vehicle as his foot collided with another officer on the other side. They had no idea he was even there. Zavier thought to himself that this is going to be easy and he wasn't wrong.

The two boys were out the door before he could even move but Ezra knew what he must do. He stepped into the doorway but was met with the blast of a gun. It threw him back twenty feet into the concrete wall, leaving it crumbling around him. From under the rubble he could hear his mother scream but it hardly registered as he stood from the rubble like a phoenix rising from the ashes. There was a piece of concrete laying on his hand, and as he stood he launched it toward the door. The soldier was hit so hard that he disappeared from the doorway like he was Zavier going invisible.

Ezra noticed the sky was beginning to turn dark as he started out the door. The drones were filling the sky to the point that it looked like the darkness of night had come early. He grabbed the closest vehicle. He didn't even know how much weight he can really carry now and he didn't even think about it. He simply crouched down, placed his hands under the van, and tossed it like it was a medicine ball. The vehicle soared through the air straight into the cloud of drones. The explosions lit the sky.

The fight only lasted about ten minutes. Drew and Heidi emerged from the school and they could see the smoke from over turned vehicles. They could see drones lying broken and shattered across the field. They could see officers littered on the ground. In the midst of the smoke and chaos stood their boys. The smoke was slowly snaking around them and the parents could see them heaving from exhaustion.

The parents knew their boys were called to do something great in that moment. They were called to be warriors. They were called to be heroes. They knew that the boys were given this gift to do more than just deliver their family. They were called to deliver the nation and maybe even the world. Drew stared at the boys with his mouth gapped open.

"Did God just call our boys to be modern day judges?"

# 7

# Some Time to Think

Azalia had slept better that night than she had in years. She had not slept in a real bed with clean sheets since the Gathering. Washing clothes became much harder with no power. The constant threat of being seen by drones was not a help either. She stretched, and almost felt guilty for feeling so content. She had a long talk with Prime Minister Treadon the night before and she was left feeling confused.

Azalia loved her family but everything she wanted and missed was right at her finger tips. She could hear car horns honking in the distance and she could hear music playing softly in another room. There was even a TV mounted on the wall in front of her and a remote a couple feet away on the bed side table. She picked it up and clicked the power button. The TV came to life and immediately she was flooded with memories of waking up before the Gathering and starting her day by watching TV. She realized in that moment that she wasn't sure that she really wanted to go home. She could really get used to this life.

Azalia began to replay the conversation with Treadon from the night before. He had spoken with her for a couple hours, asking lots of questions about life on the outside. He asked her how she managed to find food to eat. She told him that the family fished but never gave him much detail. She did not want to give away to much information and lead the government to her family.

Treadon asked Azalia if she liked living life without any of the things other people had? He told her about the movies that play in the theatre, about the hockey games at the arena, the shopping malls, and the concerts. Azalia had asked about BTS and she was informed that they had toured through the city last year. She was so excited that they still toured but was bummed out that she missed the show. He asked her if she had ever driven a car before, and when she said that she didn't know how to drive, he told her that he would take her for a drive first thing in the morning.

Azalia was replaying this conversation in her mind when something on the TV snapped her back into the present. There was a breaking news story playing. The story was about how rebels had attacked officers in the old Maritime region of the country. The camera was rotating around a cloud of smoke. As the scene cleared, what she saw sent shivers up her spine. On the screen stood the old school that her family had been living in. She scrambled to turn up the volume. The reports were that it must have been a large army of rebels. There were no vehicles left and most of the drones laid in a heap. The news reports kept replaying a 2 second clip of a soldier flying through the air and a vehicle soaring through the air and destroying the drones. It was in that moment that the camera went blank.

The reporters were sitting around a table talking about how these rebels were going to ruin their way of life if they were not taken care of. They wondered if the Government would bring in other officers from the other Capitals to end this rebellion? They even began to talk about the rebels like they would cause the reemergence of the virus. It was with that statement that Azalia wondered if the virus was still in the world? She hadn't heard any talk about a virus for years. No one, not even the odd traveller that would come through the town, had ever made a mention of it.

"We need to interrupt this talk for a moment."

The reporter on the screen was almost hysterical. It was like they were afraid yet they seemed excited about the chaos.

"There is some more footage that has just come in from the recent attacks."

The screen showed the field beside the school littered with drones and bodies but in the corner of the screen you could see movement. The camera zoomed in and there she was. Azalia's heart skipped a beat.

On the screen stood her mom. She emerged from the School and looked like she wasn't hurt. The whole scene didn't last long and the camera went black again.

"Who is this mystery woman?"

The reporters were tripping all over one another.They all tried to speak over each other to get their two cents in. The TV suddenly shut off and in the black screen Azalia could see the reflection of Treadon standing in the doorway.

"Who is she?"

Treadon sounded more stern than he did last night and Azalia knew that she needed to give him an answer.

"I am not sure what her name is but she has passed through the town before." Azalia knew that she was lying, but she needed to protect her family, and this was the only thing she could do.

"Are you aware that their existence threatens our existence?"

Treadon had thrown his smile on again and was speaking with a soft voice.

"They carry the virus. If they come here they will spread it and kill us all. You seem to see us as the enemy but we are the good guys. You were on the wrong side of the battle my dear. You will have a week to decide what you want. You can choose this life with everything you've ever dreamed, or you will be removed from this society and viewed as a threat."

He still smiled as he spoke but the words seemed threatening.

"I do not understand!"

Azalia was confused how she could be considered a threat to anyone.

"After the Virus," Treadon began to explain, "We created a vaccine that saved all mankind. The problem was that there were those who rebelled and refused the treatment. The only way to save mankind was to isolate those who refused the treatment from those who chose life."

Azalia was keenly aware that it was those living in the Capital who had isolated. It was not the rest of us. She did not feel that this was the time to correct him so she let him continue.

"Those who refused treatment were told what they were giving up by refusing the vaccine. But they couldn't accept that life was going to be different. They still wanted to live like the rest of us but without the treatments. They put us all at risk so they needed to be taken care of."

"What do you mean by 'taken care of?'"

Azalia was starting to become a little irritated.

"By what ever means possible we needed to exterminate the threat!" Treadon had now lost his smile. "I understand that this is completely different than what you have been taught but I am sure that if you will give yourself a week, you will see that this life is much more desirable than what you lived like before. It is certainly better than the alternative."

Azalia could only guess what the alternative was, but she was too afraid to ask.

"Well enough of this talk! Are we going to go for a drive?" Azalia plastered on a smile and tried to lighten the mood.

"Let's go. I've got the perfect day planned out."

Treadon's smile was back, and with that statement he turned on his heels and headed out the door.

"Are you coming or what?" He yelled back to Azalia.

"On my way!!" She yelled.

She wasn't sure what the day was going to bring, but she might as well enjoy the good things in life while she is here. What could it really hurt anyways?

The day was amazing. It was the most fun Azalia had had in years. She learned to drive, she went to eat out at an actual restaurant, Treadon gave her a tour of the city, and they even went into the concert hall. It was the biggest building she had ever been in. The walls were plastered with posters of the bands that had stopped at the city on their tour. There were so many. She had missed so much by living on the outside. That was the first time that she began to wonder if this is the life that she wanted all along? Maybe the government wasn't the bad guys at all? What if her family were rebels and they were putting everyone at risk? How could she and her family consider themselves loving if they were going to bring the return of the virus from their actions?

"You know what!" Azalia thought to herself. "I'm just going to have as much fun as I can this week and worry about it all at the end of the week."

For a moment she wondered if the family was ok but she quickly brushed the thought aside.

"This is my week. I'm not going to let anything bring me down."

# 8

# The Journey Begins

"What do you mean that we are going to just stay put?"

Heidi sounded a bit worried and maybe a little annoyed. Ezra could tell that she wasn't really on board with the decision that his father had just put forth. Drew decided at night, while everyone else was pretending to sleep, that the boys needed to track down Azalia and bring her home.

Ezra had laid awake all night trying to look like he was sleeping. He could tell that his brothers were doing the same, and he was pretty sure that his mom wouldn't be sleeping at all. Drew paced the halls of the school all night. Ezra could hear him muttering under his breath each time he passed the doorway to their room. He assumed his dad was praying. He could hear Zavier moving around a lot and Zaiden wasn't talking in his sleep, so he must be awake. All in all, it was a long night.

When they got out of bed and went to the cafeteria Drew looked like he was ready to give a speech. He did not disappoint.

"Guys, We just watched you dismantle an entire squad of officers. This is not normal. I am not going to claim that I have all the answers but I do know that you guys have some incredible abilities and gifts."

He was speaking like a war general, and the boys were his army. The boys knew that they were going to be on a mission and they felt ready.

"The government is going to come back but I think that they will be looking for an army, not just a family hidden in an old school. We have the element of surprise and we need to take advantage of this before we lose this advantage. This is what I feel we need to do; Boys! Your mom and I will stay here and make sure we keep our food source going. What you need to do is go west. You need to get to the Capital as fast as possible and you need to get Azalia out of there. I have never heard of anyone coming back from the

Capital but I do not believe that you have been given these gifts to rescue a dead girl."

That was when Heidi stood and disagreed.

"What do you mean that we are going to just stay put? You think that I'm going to let those people take all my kids? If you think that you are about to be very disappointed. There is no way I am sending my kids off to some war."

Heidi was visibly upset with the idea.

Zaiden stood as his mother was on her last word. "We can do this! We just took out 100 officers without hardly breaking a sweat. I know that we can get there mom! Let us save Azalia!" Zaiden was speaking in a way that almost sounded like he was pleading with her.

"We got this!" Ezra had joined the conversation now and he was sounding a little more forceful. "Did you just see what we did out there? I picked up a truck and threw it. Zavier was beating people up without them even knowing they were in a fight. Zaiden was running around so fast that the officers were on the ground before they realized they had been hit. Who can really stand up to us?"

Ezra was aware that the mission would be difficult, but he also knew that they had been given this gift for a reason and he was not going to let it go to waste.

"Why do we have to go alone?"

Zavier knew that the boys needed to do something but he didn't know why his parents had to stay home. "Wouldn't it be safer if you guys were with us? What are you going to do if the officers come back? If the government shows up again they are not going to be very happy." Zavier was making some good points but his dad had the answers already. It was like he had been thinking about this all night.

"We would slow you guys down."

Drew was talking less like a general and more like a father now. "You will have to look after us in battle if we go with you guys. You would be more concerned with us not being killed then being killed yourselves. You are going to face some fierce battles and you are not going to need any distractions."

Heidi was listening intently. She did not like this idea but she knew Drew was right. She loved her children, and would do anything for these kids, but she knew that the only way to bring her daughter home safely was if these boys were at their best.

"Fine."

The words almost hurt coming out of her mouth.

"If the boys are willing to go and work together, then this might be our only option to bring Azalia home."

And with that statement it was settled. The boys were about to go on the greatest journey of their lives.

The boys quickly gathered their things, hugged their parents goodbye, and set out across the old field toward the road. The boys waved goodbye as they turned one last time to look at their parents. The mission had begun and things were about to get a bit crazy. The boys held back tears from their eyes as their parents went out of view, but they knew that this must be done. The boys knew that they were the only ones capable of accomplishing this mission.

Heidi and Drew watched as their boys left their line of sight. This had been one of the hardest days either of them had ever lived. Azalia had been captured and now their boys were heading off to an impossible war.

"I hope that we are making the right decision."

Drew spoke so low that Heidi could hardly hear him. She reached her arm around him and laid her head on his shoulder.

"This is why they have the gifts they've been given. We need to trust God in this. If he calls you, he will equip you. We have to believe that."

They stared longingly in the direction of where their boys once stood just moments ago, then turned to go inside the school.

"Let's make sure that they have food fit for a warrior when they return."

Drew was scared for the boys but he knew standing and looking into the field was not going to help.

It took the boys almost an hour to walk to the other side of town. They had not been to that side of town in months. It had been a long time since they saw the old civic centre standing on the hill. It was all grown over now. Trees had grown around it and some vines looked like they were devouring the building whole. Behind the civic centre they could see the old chapel standing in the distance. It too looked like nature was taking back its lot of land.

The boys quickly realized that it was going to take months to get to the Capital at the pace they were moving. They decided that they needed to figure out how they were going to get moving a bit faster. They went down to the old hardware store and found a bicycle. They noticed one of those trailers that parents drag behind them when they want to go for a ride, but the kids are too small. They hooked the trailer up to the back of their bike and Zaiden and Zavier climbed in. Ezra was the strongest, so they figured that he would be the best one to peddle. Well, two of them agreed. Ezra wasn't so happy with the decision.

The boys had been on the road for a few hours and they were awestruck with the world around them. The old highways had grown over but the old signs could still be read if you wiped the plant growth off of them. They knew that they were going in the right direction and everything was fine until they got to the old city of Fredericton.

The Bridge crossing the river did not look too good. The cement columns underneath the bridge had mostly eroded away. It didn't look like the bridge could hold up a mouse let alone three growing boys. Unfortunately, they knew that it was the only way across the river.

"Well Zaiden," Zavier had a smirk on his face, "How about you go first."

"Why should I go first?" Zaiden was obviously not too happy about his brother's idea.

"You guys are just a bunch of wimps. I'll go first." Ezra was always the first to say he would go.

Once he stepped out onto the eroding bridge he realized that maybe someone else should have went. Part of the bridge gave way under his feet as he took his first step onto the bridge. The boys watched as the rock, that was once part of the bridge, plummeted hundreds of feet into the water. As they stood there watching the water splash below them.

"Well Ezra, you said you were going. Why aren't you going?"

Zaiden could see the swing from Ezra's hand coming and the whole world slowed once again as he went into hyper speed. He ducked under Ezra's hand and directed it towards the old concrete railing of the bridge. Zaiden's world returned to normal speed again and Ezra's hand knocked the railing right off the bridge. The boys watched again as the railing hit the water with a splash.

"Help me with this guys!"

Zavier's voice was strained, and as Ezra turned, he could see Zavier wheeling an old motorbike up the road. There was grass and bushes hanging off the bike so Ezra assumed his brother must have found it laying in the bushes.

"Guys! We are not suppose to be just standing here throwing things into the water. We are suppose to be getting to the city."

Zaiden always seemed to get annoyed with Zavier when he got distracted.

"What does it matter? It is only one thing. Just let me throw this one thing over then we can keep going."

Zavier loved to see things smashing and falling into the water. He couldn't understand what the big deal was. He could see Ezra coming from the corner of his eye. Ezra put one hand on the back the bike and gave it a shove. The boys watched as the bike soared through the air. They all realized the moment that Ezra pushed the bike, that they probably should not have done that.

Ezra listened as the boys argued over throwing something into the water. He had heard enough. He just walked up to the bike and, with maybe a little bit of frustration, shoved the bike over the edge. He knew that he had pushed too hard as soon as he pushed. The bike soared through the air, and instead of hitting the water, it hit the cement column in the middle of the river. The column that was holding the centre of the bridge.

The boys watched in disbelief as the bridge started to sway. They could hear the rock crumbling before they could start to see it crack and give way with a loud rumble. The boys watched as the bridge, that once stood as their only way over, began to descend into the river below. The boys stood looking horrified at their mistake. All except Zavier. He stood wide eyed, enjoying every moment of the action.

"Well that's great!" Irritation could be heard in Zaiden's voice.

"Wait! Look at the bridge in the river!" Zavier was so excited that it looked like he was going to jump off the bridge. "The bridge landed perfectly flat. If we break the next column over then we could walk across the bridge. The water would only be shallow. Only our feet would get wet."

The idea was a good one and the boys went down the steep embankment to the river side. Ezra picked up a tree that had recently fallen and threw it as hard as he could. The tree made direct contact on the first try. The column shook, and just like the one before, it came crashing down. The boys took their bike and waded across the river. They were full of confidence when they reached the other side of the river. They had had their first obstacle and they got by it like a piece of cake. This was not going to be hard at all.

"Give me your bags! While you are at it, I kind of like that bike too."

Ezra knew that the voice wasn't either of his brothers, and as he turned, he was greeted by a baseball bat to the side of the head. The bat splintered the moment it made contact and the man on the other side of the bat stood in disbelief. Ezra smirked back.

The moment the man started to speak, Zavier's whole world went blank and white as he went invisible. He could see at least ten figures glowing, besides those of his brothers. He swung with all his might and connected with the throat of the nearest figure to him. The man crumbled with a soft whimper. Zavier could tell that the figures shifted focus to their fallen comrade as soon as he hit the ground. Zavier saw Zaiden suddenly move at, what seemed like, the speed of light.

Zaiden was looking at Zavier when they heard the man speak. Zavier was suddenly gone. He simply vanished in thin air. It wasn't a second later, and

Zaiden watched as one of the men collapsed in a heap with a soft whimper. Zaiden knew that the fight was on!

His world slowed as he entered hyper speed once again. He watched the other men move in slow motion and he noticed that they were all equipped with bats or knives. Some had their faces covered and most of them had back packs on. He knew that these men had one intention. These men wanted to rob the brothers. Zaiden knew that he wasn't about to let that happen as he approached his first opponent.

The first man Zaiden came to was looking at his friend laying on the ground, and the look on his face was one of disbelief. That look went from disbelief to shock, and then pain. Zaiden swept his feet from under him, then Zaiden's world went back to normal speed. Zaiden forced his elbow into the gut of the robber as the man was still mid air. The body was hitting the ground and flat on his back when Zaiden's world slowed once again. He lunged towards the next victim and kicked the side of his knee. The man was falling before he even knew he had been hit. Swinging around, Zaiden landed a round house kick to the robber.

Zaiden was planting his feet to make his next move when he could see something coming toward him from the corner of his eye. It was the body of one of the other robbers flying through the air. The body was coming straight at him.

He slipped under the flying body and he noticed Ezra a few feet away. Two men were on Ezra's back, yet he was holding two other men in the air by the throat. Each in one hand.

Ezra smirked as soon as the bat made contact with his head.

"Was that suppose to hurt?" Ezra teased.

He grabbed the man by the throat and picked him up. He tossed him to the side like he was a baseball. Two other men jumped on his back and two others came straight at him. The first man lunged at him with a knife. Ezra grabbed at him but the man ducked around the attack and attempted to plunged the knife into the skin of Ezra. It sounded like two pieces of metal colliding when the knife hit his skin. The knife glanced off and the mans wrist twisted and snapped upon impact.

Ezra took the two men in his hands and clapped them together like a pair of cymbals. The men lay motionless before him. He reached over his back and grabbed the other two men. He threw them off his shoulders like they weighed nothing. One man hit a tree and fell to the ground while the other man soared through the air. Zaiden appeared out of no where and round house kicked the flying man to the ground. The two brothers stood staring at one another.

"Well that was fun!" Zavier spoke as he appeared out of thin air between them.

"So are we going to keep going or are we just going to stand here and stare?" Zaiden and Ezra knew that Zavier was pumped up. He could do this all day.

"We should see if there is anything we can use. Check for food in their back packs. It's not like they are going to be needing them." Zaiden was smiling as he spoke.

If Zaiden was honest with himself, he actually enjoyed this. This was going to be a fun journey. Ezra spoke up as the boys gathered some food from the back packs.

"I don't want to run the bike. Can someone else do it for a while?"

"I'll bike for a little bit but I'm not going to do it the whole way." Zaiden spoke first. Ezra and Zavier slipped into the little trailer and Zaiden on the bike.

Zaiden's world slowed as he started to peddle. He had slipped into hyper-speed. He looked behind him and could see the brothers sitting in the trailer. Their hair was blowing back and their skin was flapping on their face. The fear on their face is what really entertained Zaiden.

"This is going to be fun." Zaiden spoke through a wide smile.

The old road was in pretty bad shape and there were lots of trees and plants growing. It was hard to imagine that there was once a steady flow of traffic on these roads. Zaiden simply zig zagged around the obstacles and watched joyfully as his brothers looked like they were going to be sick from the movements. Zaiden knew the boys were going to get to the city in no time at this pace.

It only took, what seemed like a few minutes, and Zaiden stopped peddling. The boys stood beside a large river. What stood on the other side of this river took their breath away. It was one of the biggest cities they had ever seen. The boys knew that this wasn't the city they were looking for though. This city was a city of ruins. Ezra got out of the trailer and walked to the side of the road. There was an old sign that stated the the name of the city clearly.

"Welcome to Montreal."

# 9

# A City at War

Montreal was different than the towns and cities the boys had passed on their journey up to this point. Instead of the deafening silence that they experienced from most of the settlements, they could hear noise coming from the ruins of this city. It sounded like gunfire and yelling. Ezra could see something coming in the water as his brothers joined him at the river bank. It became clear that it was a group of people as the object began to take shape. Some of the people were bleeding, some were crying, some were cradling their injured arms, but all had the same look of fear and despair.

Before the small raft could reach the shore, and before the boys made first contact, a voice yelled from the small structure.

"Turn around now!! Run for your lives!"

The Boys looked at one another and Zavier spoke first.

"Run from what?" Ezra knew that tone in his brother's voice. It sounded as if Zavier was offended that this group of people thought that they were going to tell him what he should do.

"It's the government!!" The man, now standing at the front of the makeshift raft, was yelling frantically.

"We thought we could form a resistance and storm the capital. We thought that there was enough of us but we were no match." The man's voice began to lower as it became clear that he was speaking from the place of defeat.

"Yesterday we saw the sky turn black from the innumerable amount of drones in the air. It was only a short time later and we got word from our scouts that there was a large army of enforcement officers entering the city. They must have spotted us because they knew exactly where to come find us. We fought hard, and it seemed like we were going to have the upper hand, but then they just kept coming. When we didn't think there could be any more officers, more would show up."

"What is the noise we are hearing? Are the offices still in the city?" Ezra had heard enough and Zaiden could tell what Ezra was thinking before he said any more. Ezra turned to look at his brothers.

"Maybe they are still transporting Azalia! She could be in there. We need to get over there and find out what's going on. We can't just stand here and watch as these people get slaughtered."

"This is not our fight. We are not here to rescue this resistance. We are coming all this way to rescue Azalia. I just want to get this done and go home." Zavier was not convinced that Ezra's idea was the best option.

"What do you mean that we are not here for this reason?" Zaiden snapped at his brother.

"We have these gifts and I really don't think that we have these abilities to just save one person. I think we need to go over there and help. Who knows? Maybe Ezra is right and Azalia is in there."

Zavier was not happy and voiced his disapproval one more time. As the survivors filed off of the raft the three boys piled on.

"What do you guys really think you can do? There are only three of you but hundreds of officers." The man, now standing on the shore watching the boys push out into the water, did not sound very encouraging.

"We are not sure what we can do, but we know what we can't do." Zaiden was getting a little frustrated with this man, who seemingly was satisfied with defeat.

"What we can't do is stand here and watch as innocent people are killed." With those last words, the boys gave one last push off from the shore and turned their attention toward the city.

The sounds of screams and gunfire became louder as the boys drifted closer to the city. They could see lights flashing between the ruins of what used to be beautiful tall buildings. The buildings were now just a shell of their former beauty. They were void of windows and had grown over with vegetation. Every flash of light from the city was followed by a loud rumble.

The boys knew that the government meant business. The government was going to end this resistance and they were going to use every bit of firepower they had. It appeared that even explosives were not out of the question. The boys neared the shore and they could hear the familiar sound of a drone over head.

"We are completely exposed out here!" Zavier spoke as he was paddling as hard as he could.

"If they see us here we are sitting ducks." Zavier could see the shore and he knew that they would reach it in a few minutes. He feared that with this drone now watching them, they did not have the time they needed.

The boys began to hear something that sounded almost like a whistle. At first it sounded like a faint sound, but it kept getting louder and louder. The boys looked at each other in recognition. They all knew that the sound was coming right for them. They looked up as the sound became defining, and just before impact, they realized that their little raft was about to meet a big bomb.

The bomb hit the raft and sent debris and fire everywhere. What was once a few pieces of lumber thrown together, was now nothing but charred wood. The boys were no where to be seen. The drone circled the wreckage a couple times and then quickly headed back toward the inner city. Its mission was accomplished.

The boys looked up as the sound of the approaching bomb became deafening. Zaiden's whole world slowed as he saw the bomb about to hit their tiny raft. He leapt toward Ezra and kicked him square in the the middle of his shoulders. The impact sent Ezra flying into the air and into the water.

Zaiden used Ezra's body for leverage and pushed off towards the water on the other side of the raft. He wrapped his arm around Zavier, as he passed, and dragged him into the water with him.

Zaiden could hear the explosion from under water and he was pushed back in the waves. His head breached the surface of the water with a gasp of breath. He could see the drone heading back toward the city.

Ezra had no idea what had just happened. He was standing and looking at a bomb that was about to hit him square on the forehead. The next thing he remembered was coming up for air from under the water. As he swam toward the shore he could see his brothers swimming a little distance away. They all seemed to be heading in the same direction. He saw Zavier's hand lift from the water and give a quick wave. The brothers were safe but this fight was far from over. This fight was just starting and now they were mad.

Zavier was the first to shore. He was also the first to speak as he and his brothers stood soaked to the bone.

"I've had enough. They took our sister, they attacked our parents, and now they have tried to kill us. It's time that we take care of this."

Zavier was more focused than he had ever been in his life. They came with a mission to save their sister, but now they are going to make sure that no one ever looses a loved one again to these people. The boys didn't say another word. They simply walked. They walked straight to the drones. They walked straight to the officers. They walked straight to the armoured vehicles. They walked straight to the war.

The city was dark but the boys knew exactly where they were going. They tried to stay low and out of sight but there was no hiding where they were going. They could see the flashes of light getting brighter and the sounds of battle were getting louder. As the boys rounded a building, that seemed like an old arena, they came face to face with a sword. The point of the sword rested on the throat of Zaiden.

"Who are you?"

The voice was forceful but seemed short of breath. Whoever this was sounded like they had been running from someone or something. The blade pressed harder into Zaiden's throat, and with slight pressure up, the man used the blade to lift Zaiden's head.

"I asked you a question!" The man was now shouting.

Zaiden heard Zavier speak before he had a chance to react.

"I'm Zavier and these are my brothers Ezra and Zaiden. We are here to help you if you are not officers. If you are officers, then I apologize a head of time for the beating we are about to lay on you."

Zaiden could feel the pressure from the blade ease and he could see a slight smirk cross the face of the man holding the sword.

"I used to know three brothers with the same name," the man started. "I used to live on the east coast and we used to hang out when we were kids. My brother and I got taken in the first Gathering, and I have't seen them since. My name is Auston. My brother and I run this resistance."

Zaiden pushed the blade aside.

"Are you kidding me! Auston, it's us! The government took Azalia so we are heading to the capital to get her back. How did you guys end up here? I thought all those gathered were given the choice to join the city or die?"

The boys could not believe that they were standing with their old friend.

"Where is Mitchell?" Ezra was looking forward to reuniting with his old friend.

"We got separated in the fighting. I would assume that he is over in that direction. Where the fighting is going on. I do not think he will be able to hold off the officers if we don't get there soon. There are so many officers. We have never seen so many before."

The boys could hear the discouragement in his voice and they knew that they needed to step in and fight.

"Stay here!"

Ezra was already in a full run before he even waited to see if Auston and his men were going to listen to his command. He could see his brothers running beside him as he circled the building and into a cloud of smoke. As long as they were in this together, there was no enemy that could defeat them. Not even the entire weight of the government and it's military. The boys stepped out of the cloud of smoke and into the middle of a fight.

There were bullets and beams of light from the pulse guns flying in every direction. Ezra could see a large tank with its pulse cannon pointed straight at a group of people. Ezra could only assume that this group was the resistance. He ran straight at the machine and pushed the barrel of the gun skyward. He had arrived just in time as the tank was firing another round. The beam of light shot from the barrel of the tank and straight into the drones over head. The explosions of the drones lit the sky.

Zaiden saw Ezra running for the large machine and his world slowed as he entered hyper-speed. He could see officers moving to surround the resistance fighters, so he sped forward in their direction. Zaiden arrived to the group of people as an officer pointed his gun barrel at a freedom fighter. Zaiden kicked the gun from the officers hands, spun around, and made a bone crunching blow to the officers head with the back of his fist. Zaiden's world went back to normal speed for a moment, as the officer hit the ground in a heap.

"Run!!" Zaiden screamed at the resistance and he turned his attention to the other officers.

Zaiden's world slowed once again as he entered hyper-speed. He swept the feet from underneath another soldier. He used his lifeless body as a spring board and he leapt toward the other three offices. The officers had no idea what was happening. One minute they stood, seemingly having the upper hand, then the next moment they were laying lifeless and unresponsive on the ground.

Zaiden had reached the first officer in the air. He slammed the officer's head against the wall as he lunged toward the other officers standing nearby. He kicked the knee out of the first officer, and as the officer was falling, Zaiden took hold of his arm and swung him toward the remaining officer. When the officer hit the other one, knocking him to the ground, Zaiden leapt on top of him. The world once again returned to normal speed and the officer looked terrified.

"Lights out!"

Zaiden laid a solid punch to the officer's forehead and knocked him out. Zaiden looked across the street where Ezra was fighting and he could see a soldier firing his weapon toward his own people. Zaiden thought that Zavier must be doing his thing. Zaiden turned his eyes to more unsuspecting victims and continued his fight.

Zavier knew that the fight was on as he watched his brothers run in opposite directions towards the battle. Zavier's world went black and white as be became invisible. There were so many glowing figures that he couldn't count. He hoped that they had not just stepped into a fight that they could not win. He could see the officers in Zaiden's direction falling like flies. He could see drones falling from the sky as Ezra had directed the gun fire skyward. It was in that moment he recognized a big problem.

Zavier could see an endless glow of human bodies streaming in from every direction. He quickly ran toward the resistance soldiers that had bunkered down for the fight.

"We need to get out of here!" He appeared in front of those soldiers and they must have thought that he was a ghost from the terrified look on their face.

"We don't have all day! Trust me, I'm going to get you out of here."

Zavier led the group through the gun fire. They tried to stay low but it was no use. The officers just kept coming. Zavier would periodically vanish, only to reappear behind officers. Throwing them aside and dispatching of them with well placed blows. The group knew that he was on their side and kept close. He led them from the battle and out of harm.

"I have to go back for my brothers. Auston and the others are down the road. They will meet you there. Stay low and under cover. We will see you again soon. This is just getting good." With his final words, and a smile to ease the fear, Zavier vanished once again.

The fight raged on for hours. Ezra was throwing officers through the air and he was punching and kicking them and sending them flying hundreds of feet. He had been stabbed a few times but it was like the blades just glanced off of his skin.

Zaiden was moving at the speed of light and was dispatching the enemy before they had a chance to defend themselves.

Zavier couldn't be seen but the brothers could see officers firing guns into the air randomly and other officers firing at one another. In the midst of the chose of the battle they could see bodies dropping like flies. The brothers knew that Zavier was the cause of such confusion.

The three boys stood in a circle when the fight had finally ended. They stood motionless as the smoke circled around them. A few groans could be heard from fallen enemies, but for the first time since they entered the city, there was mostly silence.

They turned their attention down the street as they could hear another group coming.

"When will this ever end? I just want to rest." Zavier sighed aloud.

A familiar face began to take shape out of the smoke.

"Mitchell?" Ezra's voice carried with it the sound of exhaustion but also relief.

"We have a lot to talk about old friend." Mitchell was dirty and bloody, but a smile emerged on the face of the man that just endured an exhausting battle.

"Let's grab a bite to eat. I think you've all earned a meal."

# 10

# A Reunion of Old Friends

The boys had so much to talk about. They remembered their hockey games together and hanging out when they were kids. Most of the conversation centred around The Gathering. The boys had been hanging out the day before their world changed and life seemed to be as normal as one could expect in those days. When the raid began on Sussex everyone searched for a place to hide. Ezra and his two brothers lived through it and survived, but what their friends told them sent a wave of emotion through their minds.

"We went home that night and had every intention of coming back over to your place in the morning." Mitchell was speaking in a low somber voice.

"We woke up to our parents dragging us from our beds. They were speaking in a whisper but we could see the urgency and fear in their eyes. We knew that something was terribly wrong."

"I remember when we first heard the footsteps in the kitchen." Auston was picking up the story now, and the intensity in his voice was not lost on the brothers.

"Dad put his finger to his lips to signal us to be quiet, and then he stepped out the door. Mom was holding me back because I was trying to follow dad out the door. She just wouldn't let me go. Dad had left the door open a crack and I could see two men standing in the kitchen. Dad asked them who they were (as if he didn't know from the uniforms they were wearing), but they told him it didn't matter who they were. The officer told my dad that he and his family were coming with them. Dad told them it was only him living there but one of the men clicked something on his arm and a holographic image emerged from a small box. It was a video from the day before when we were outside gathering berries from a bush on our property."

Zaiden noticed that Mitchell was starting to shift in his seat as the story was getting uneasy for him to hear. Auston noticed as well and paused but Mitchell signalled his brother to keep going.

"Dad tried to deny that we were still here but the deception was met with a swift blow to the head. Dad didn't see it coming and fell to the ground. I tried to get up but mom was still holding me back. I twisted and turned until I broke free. The officers heard the commotion before I exited the door and the moment I stepped out from the room one of the soldiers opened fire. It was only one shot but mom was following me out the door and threw herself between me and the bullet."

Auston paused for a moment and the brothers could see the tears forming in his eyes.

"They just killed her. Right there in front of her children, the officer took her life. There was nothing we could do. It was like they had no heart. They only had a mission." Auston collected himself and continued.

"Dad screamed for mom but when he tried to get up he was met with another hit. This time the barrel of a gun was pointed right at him. The officer told him that if he moved he would end up like his wife. I can remember the officer smirking and telling my dad to try and get up. He told my dad that the less people they had to transfer back to the Capital the better. Unfortunately dad accepted his invitation."

"Mitchell and I tied to help mom but it was too late. She was already gone. As we were laying over her body dad rose to his feet in defiance. He was barely on his knees and I saw the second shot go off and my dad laying on the floor. The officers didn't care that we just lost our parents. They didn't care that we were still young kids. They just knew that we needed to be gathered to the Capital. They drug us out of our home without even letting us say goodbye to our parents."

Auston's voice lowered and his eyes narrowed.

"They will regret ever coming to Sussex."

"I'm so sorry to hear about your family!"

Zaiden was sitting with tears in his eyes and wondered to himself if his parents were ok. He wondered if the government had returned to find them. This thought was interrupted by the sound of Zavier's voice beside him.

"How did you end up here fighting in this city? Did you get away from the government before they got you into the truck?"

Zavier was wondering if there was something that they could learn here that would assist them in getting their sister back. He felt bad for his friends but he still had a mission. He and his brothers needed to save his own family.

"We had no hope of escaping the government." Mitchell was now speaking in a tone that was once again that of a leader rallying his troops.

"We were thrown in the truck with about 20 other people. They played soft music and talked to us like they were there to be our friends. They told us of the wonderful life that awaited us in the Capital. We were coming through Montreal when we heard screaming, from what sounded like a thousand people. I heard one of the officers say something in his radio about the resistance and he cocked his gun. Before he even got out of the back of the truck the doors swung open and a group of people stood there. They were dirty, bloodied, but focused on one thing. Getting us out of there."

"They stormed the trucks that had been carrying us prisoners, or as the government likes to call us, future members of the Capital. They took out all the officers and took their weapons, communication devises, and then disabled the trucks. They left the trucks where they had stopped. The resistance told us that it was because if they kept blocking off the government's planned routes, then the resistance could control the flow of traffic through the city. It gave them an upper hand. They aimed the weapons skyward and shot every drone in sight. The resistance figured that if we take their ability to travel and their ability to see what's going on in here, then we isolate them in their own Capital. They would be blind to what is happening here and they will be sitting ducks when we storm the Capital one day."

Mitchell sounded quite confident that they would be able to storm the Capital one day but Ezra wasn't so sure.

Mitchell and Auston had seen the boys gifts during the battle and they tried to convince them to join the resistance. The boys were not interested in joining a resistance. They were not here to fight a war. The brothers were here to get their sister back.

The question of how they were able to do what they can do came up. The boys explained the prayer and discovery of their gifts. They told the story of losing their sister and shared their mission with the resistance. They all agreed that they were on the same side but had different missions. They said their goodbyes, got a quick bite to eat, and then the boys set out for the Capital. As they left their friends, they wondered to one another if Azalia was ok. They thought it was better not to think about it and just keep pressing forward.

****************

Behind the beautiful walls, the lovely buildings, and the manicured lawns, stood Treadon. He gazed into the tv screen as the replay of the recent battle was being viewed. The rebels had been in Montreal for too long. The citizens of the Capital were waking up this morning and seeing that the rebellion was getting a strong hold. If he allowed them to make it to the city gates the virus could be with them. If the fighting didn't kill his citizens the virus would. That was at least the story that every news broadcast was carrying. As long as the rebels were seen as a threat, the people would stand behind his response no matter how violent and decisive his plan. This was not the major concern for him this morning though. There was something else that seemed unexplainable but was of grave concern.

Treadon awoke to a knock on his door in the early hours of the morning. One of his followers entered and passed him a tablet. He watched footage from the battle in Montreal that had taken place the night before. He was the first to see the incredible footage captured from the drones. What caught his eye was this one fighter. He seemed to just disappear into thin air. He watched as the bodies of his offices were falling and then this fighter would simply reappear once again. He watched the video several times before he addressed the man standing by his bedside.

"Edit that footage out. No one is to see that footage. We need to figure out who this is and how this is possible. He must be stopped, or at the very least, given the opportunity to join the right side."

With the wave of his hand hand Treadon dismissed the man standing next to him.

A few hours had passed since that bedside meeting and now the world was seeing the footage of the dangerous rebels. Treadon picked up his tablet and mirrored the image to his TV screen. He began to play the unedited version once again. How was he going to find this fighter? When he did, how was he going to convince him to fight on his side. He was so intent on staring at the screen that he didn't even notice someone step up behind him.

"Zavier?"

Treadon turned to see who had interrupted his private moment. Azalia was standing just behind him staring at the screen intently. This girl knew the fighter.

"You know this man?" Treadon was trying not to sound too eager.

"That's my brother! What's going on? Why is he on your TV?"

Treadon knew that this was the best news he could have received. It had become more clear than ever that this girl must be made a citizen. This girl was the advantage he needed to convince this incredible man to join his army. Treadon knew that a man with the ability to vanish would make his officers unstoppable. Now he just needed to convince this foolish girl to join the Capital. Let the game begin.

# 11

## Temptations

"What was my brother doing?"

Azalia had seen Zavier on Treadon's screen and wanted answers. She hadn't seen her family in days and wondered if they were even alive. Now she walks by Treadon's room and sees her brother on his TV screen? Something was going on here and she wanted answers.

"Have a seat Azalia."

Treadon was speaking in a calm demeanour with his smile still plastered on his face. His eyes began to soften and he spoke in a voice full of concern.

"Last night there was an attack on our officers. They were trying to disperse those living in Montreal. With so much fear of this virus still being out there, everyone must do their part to ensure that the virus doesn't spread. If the virus spreads in that city and one of our officers got it, they would carry it to the Capital. An outbreak of the virus would threaten to put an end to everything we've worked so hard to maintain here."

Azalia wasn't sure what this had to do with her brothers. She wasn't all that concerned with anything else at this point.

"That's all well and good, but what does this have to do with Zavier?"

Azalia noticed that Treadon's smile shifted for just a moment but then he regained his composure. She realized that she had spoken a bit more forceful than she intended but she wouldn't apologize to this man.

"This footage," Treadon continued, "is from the battle last night. Most of our men did not return. Their families are now being notified. You've been raised to believe that you are on the right side of this fight but what if you are wrong? How is it right that those families have to be notified today that they've lost their loved ones? How is it right that, because of a few people, our way of life is threatened and we have to live in fear?"

Azalia had never thought of it that way before. She began to wonder if her family really was the problem? What if all this time she could have been enjoying music and movies? She could have been going out with friends and driving in cars like she used to? Her tone changed and it softened towards Treadon as she spoke once again.

"So how is my brother involved in all this?"

"It would seem that your brother has joined the rebel cause." Treadon was turning to look at the screen as he spoke.

"I understand that he is your brother and you have a lot of conflicting emotions right now but you must think of our people. You have an opportunity to be part of this society, and these will be your people as well. It is the duty of every citizen to keep one another safe."

As he turned to look at Azalia once again he looked straight into her eyes as he sat down beside her.

"I think you know what you should do. Join with us and live a life that you've dreamed of. Live a life free from fear and poverty. I will personally take you to the medical centre if you will come with me now."

"Why would I need to go to the medical centre?"

Azalia couldn't believe that she was even considering this, but no one here seemed to be unhappy. Everyone seemed to be enjoying life. Why shouldn't she be able to be like everyone else for once?

"We needed to apply some safety measures in the other Capitals around the world." Treadon's posture was changing and Azalia could hear the excitement in his voice. "We fit each citizen with a chip that allows us to check your vital signs on command so that you can just live your life without worry. We can tell if you just have a common cold, if your blood pressure is high, or if you have contracted the virus. It helps us to achieve a safe society. The chip also helps us locate you in case you get lost or injured. We are able to send drones straight to your location and offer assistance."

This seemed so high tech to Azalia, and a little scary, but that was probably because of what her mom and Drew had taught her. Everyone else seemed fine and happy. She listened as Treadon continued.

"We no longer need physical currency as long as we have this chip. When you go to your place of employment, that we will assign to you, you simply walk through a scanner. You will receive your pay immediately into your account. This makes it impossible for pay to be withheld from you by an employer, to lose your money, or have your money stolen. The chip is scanned whenever you board a plan to travel to another Capital as well. This is to ensure that we are able to keep you safe. These measures are in place in case of an international incident or natural disaster."

This sounded nothing like what Azalia had been taught. This sounded great!

"I hope you understand that there is another side to this as well Azalia." Treadon's tone was changing to something a little more serious. It was a slight shift from the excitement earlier.

"We must all agree to live in harmony to keep everyone safe. No one must be permitted through those security gates without a chip. This is for the safety of all citizens. We must all agree to live as one and abide by the rules we have provided. If we all live like this we can continue to thrive as a people. The entire society that we have worked hard to achieve could come crashing down if there is one bad apple. This is why the rebels are so dangerous. They refuse to live by our rules. I hope you understand that we must end the rebellion before it grows into something that threatens us all."

Azalia understood what he was telling her. The moment had arrived and she needed to make a choice. Was she going to be a part of this thriving society or would she continue to live like a rebel and face the consequences of that choice. She looked at her brother on the screen one more time before turning to Treadon. She knew the choice she was making but she felt she deserved happiness too.

"Let's go to the medical centre. I'm ready for my new life."

The TV went dark as Treadon clicked it off. Azalia could see the smile on his face as he was turning toward the door. She finally felt like she was going to be part of something special. This was going to be a new adventure and she could hardly wait to see what was coming. She wondered briefly how her mom and Drew would react, or how her brothers might be effected, but she quickly brushed the thought aside. Today was about finding her happiness and no one was going to stop her.

# 12

# Silence the Wind

It was getting quite late and Zavier wanted to stop. The boys had been traveling for a long time. It had been almost a day since they left Montreal and his feet were starting to get sore. He just wanted to go home to his mom and dad and just have a normal day again. The boys had come across a river earlier in the day and that added a little fun to their journey. They thought they would take a minute to rest and throw some rocks into the water. It turned into a competition on who could skip their rock the furthest. Ezra threw a rock so hard that it stuck into a tree on the other side of the river. Zaiden threw one so fast that the boys had no idea where it went. They decided that it would only be fair if they didn't use their gifts. Zaiden still won their little competition but Zavier was convinced that it was because he had used his gift. They began to argue and then walked on for several hours before anyone would even talk again. Zavier thought to himself that it was just like when we they home. He would give anything to be back home again.

After the argument at the water Zaiden hadn't said a word. It had been hours and his mind was racing. At first he was just frustrated with his brothers but after a short time his mind went to their mission. How were we going to get into the Capital? When they are there, how are we going to find Azalia? Is his mom and dad still ok or did the officers return to the school and capture them? Zaiden could not shake the uneasy thoughts. He looked to his brothers and wondered if they were even the slight bit concerned with how things were going to turn out.

Ezra had been keeping an eye on Zaiden for the last hour or so. His face was getting all wrinkly on his forehead like it does when he gets frustrated. He knew that his brother was being bothered by something but he wasn't sure he wanted to ask. He really didn't want to get into another big argument over something stupid like skipping rocks. He had been trying to figure out how they were going to find Azalia when they got to the Capital. He imagined that the Capital must be huge if everyone in the country was living there. He was busy trying to formulate a plan when a sound interrupted his thoughts. His brothers had noticed it as well because they had a similar look of confusion on their face.

Zavier had heard the humming sound earlier but it was really low. He thought he was just hearing something so he didn't bother saying anything to his brothers. The sound got louder the further the boys had walked but now there was a new sound added to the humming. It sounded like a swishing sound. It wasn't really anything he had heard before and he wondered out loud if his brothers had any ideas?

The three brothers stopped walking for a moment so they could hear the new sound over the crunching of rocks under their feet. Zaiden was the first to speak.

"Do you think that it is a new kind of drone?" Zaiden really had no idea what it could be but he thought he would break the silence with the guess.

"It's not moving toward us, we are moving toward it."

Ezra spoke in a quiet voice that was almost a whisper. He was sure that whatever the sound was, it wasn't anything that meant them harm.

"I've never heard anything like it before. What ever it is, it sounds like there is more than one." Ezra wasn't sure what they should do but he knew that they couldn't stop moving. "Let's keep going! We will have to stay low and make sure that we are being quiet."

The boys continued to walk and the sound got louder with every step. They had walked until the sound was so loud that they could not even hear each other speak. They stepped through a bush and what stood before them was nothing they had ever dreamed existed.

There was large windmills for as far as their eyes could see. Their large arms could be seen swinging in the night sky under the glow of the moon. What the boys saw beyond the windmills was what they had been waiting to see for days. It was the glow of the Capital. They couldn't see the buildings but nothing in nature could produce that kind of light.

"If we walk across this field we are going to be exposed during the day!" Zaiden was trying to be quiet but he was yelling because of the loud sound of the windmills.

"We won't be able to hear the drones or any of the other government vehicles and they will be able to surprise us. What are we going to do?"

"I think that we should just walk right across."

Zavier was tired of this journey and he just wanted to get Azalia and go home. "We have fought a few times now and nothing has been able to stop us yet. What is the worst that could happen? If they capture us then we will be taken inside and we will just find a way to escape." Zavier thought to himself that he was coming up with a pretty good plan the more he talked.

"That's the worst plan I've ever heard!"

Ezra was pretty sure that Zavier was making his plan up while he was speaking and it was beginning to show.

"We need to do this in a way that no one has any idea that we are coming. The element of surprise is going to be what gives us the extra advantage we need to win this battle and bring Azalia home."

"Stay where you are at! Don't move a muscle!"

Zaiden felt the cold barrel of a gun pressed against the back of his head. Ezra was still trying to finish telling the brothers his plan, oblivious to what was happening. Zaiden looked around and could tell that there were a lot of officers. Though it was quite dark out, and the officers where wearing black, he could see their silhouette in the moon's glow.

"Zavier's plan it is!"

As the words were escaping his lips, Zaiden looked toward Zavier and noticed that his brother was no longer standing where he once was.

Zavier saw the barrel press against his brother's head and before the officer even spoke. Zavier's world went black and white as he went invisible. The glow of the bodies could be seen quite easily and he knew that there were only a dozen officers. He thought to himself that this was going to be easy but he barely got the thought out of his mind when something caught his eye. It was a line of trucks heading right toward them.

Each truck was going to be filled with officers. Zavier knew that he needed to get his brothers and get out of here before it was too late. Suddenly his plan didn't sound all that appealing. He reached over and grabbed the barrel of the gun. He moved it off of his brother's head and pointed straight at an officer standing behind Ezra. The officer on the other end of the barrel pulled the trigger and the officer behind Ezra fell. The fight was on and they better make this one go fast.

The shot grazed Ezra's head as it passed by him and made contact with the officer standing behind him. Ezra thought that is was a little close for comfort but he brushed the thought aside and leap toward the officer beside him. The officer saw the movement and pushed his punch aside, kneeled down and took the feet out from underneath Ezra. He hit the ground with a thump. The officer lifted his foot and brought it down with enough force to knock out a normal man, but Ezra was not a normal man. As the officers boot made contact with Ezra's face he grabbed the officers foot with both hands and twisted. He heard the snap of bone and heard the cry of pain. Ezra stood, grabbed the man, and tossed him aside like he was a weed being picked from the garden. The man soared through the air and collided with some other officers. All three of them laid motionless. Ezra glanced over to where Zaiden was standing and he could see two officers laying on the ground. A third was being thrown to the ground by Zaiden.

Zaiden's world slowed the moment the shot was fired, as he entered hyper-speed. He could see the barrel that once pressed against the back of his head. It was now beside him and pointing in Ezra's direction. Zaiden dropped, holding the hand of the soldier that was firmly gripping the barrel of the gun, and he flipped the officer over his shoulders. The officer hit the ground and was met with a mouth full of fist. Zaiden could see a few officers bent over from what looked like a gut punch. Zaiver must have given them a good punch before they even knew he was there. Zaiden ran and jumped toward them with his knee extended. The officers, who were bent in a perfect row, all had a knee to the side of their head before they even knew what was happening.

The three boys stood in a circle looking at each other. The bodies of their attackers were now laying at their feet. They all looked to the direction of the city. What stood between the boys and the city was a large group of trucks. The trucks were speeding toward them, full of soldiers, and they needed a plan now.

Ezra looked to the sky, and was beginning to pray for guidance, when the windmill caught his eye. He stood at the bottom of the large structure and began to push. At first there was nothing. It was like he was trying to move an unmovable object. He felt a little foolish and wondered what it must look like to his brothers. That was when he heard the voice of his brothers behind him.

"Come on Ezra! You got this! Keep going! You can do this!!"

Zavier had this feeling of defeat overwhelm him as he looked toward the army of trucks headed his way. He had no idea how they were going to be able to win this fight. Sure they had some special gifts but there was too many officers. The thought had barely entered his mind when Ezra began to lean against the windmill beside him. He could see the veins beginning to pop out in his forehead and his arms were pulsating. The windmill wasn't moving. He could see a flash of discouragement cross the face of Ezra and Zavier knew what he needed to do.

"You Got this Ezra! Keep going!"

Zaiden wasn't sure how they were going to beat these officers but he was convinced that he wasn't going to die here in this field. God did not send them on this mission just to die mere miles from their destination. Zaiden was trying to formulate a game plan when he saw Ezra lean against the windmill. Surly he didn't think he was strong enough to move something that big did he? He heard Zavier starting to shout encouragement but he wasn't sure they should be waisting their time on this. Especially not when there had to be a better plan. He was trying to come up with a good idea when he first noticed a bolt begin to lift from the bracket holding the windmill to the ground.

"You can do this!!" Zaiden began to shout at his brother. He couldn't believe what he was seeing. This was going to be amazing.

Ezra was sure that he could feel movement. His brothers were shouting and he could see the trucks inching closer with every second that passed. He heard a snap and he felt the windmill shift under his push. This was actually working! Ezra, now with his confidence growing, planted his feet and let out a loud grunt as he pushed with all his might. The windmill began to make creaking sounds and other sounds that resembled a groan. The large structure began to tip and Ezra knew that it was coming down.

"Run!!"

Era shouted at his brothers as the windmill gave up the fight and began to lean and twist.

The Windmill began to fall toward the direction of the oncoming trucks. It didn't fall far before it made contact with a neighbouring windmill. The wings collided, snapped, and were sent flying. The boys began to dodge the large arms as they collided one after another. They frantically ran as the windmills were falling like dominos. One by one the windmills fell in a shower of wings and fire. The boys could see the trucks trying to turn around but it was too late for them. It was happening too fast and there was no where to go. The windmills fell on the trucks as the night sky was being lit by explosions. The boys looked beyond the field toward the city as plumes of fire ascended into the air. Suddenly, like someone had just flicked a switch, the city went dark.

"I guess we just lost the element of surprise." Zaiden was trying to be funny but his brother's didn't see the humour in it.

"I think we need to get in the city while the power is out. It might be our best chance." Zaiden was sure that this was an opportunity they could not pass up.

It was like who ever flipped the switch, to turn the lights off in the city, couldn't make up their mind and turned the lights right back on. The lights were only out for a few moments and then they flickered back to life.

"Well... I guess that didn't last long."

Again the brothers didn't find Zaiden very funny.

The boys didn't have long to enjoy their victory. They needed to get into that city. They took one last look at the field of debris and headed toward the city. Azalia was there somewhere and they were not leaving without her.

# 13

# The Home Stretch

It had been a few days since Azalia went to the medical centre. She had been told for years that it was this scary place and that horrible experiments were done there. This was not the case at all. When she had arrived at the centre she was greeted with a smile. There were all sorts of encouraging posters on the walls. The nurses welcomed her in and even escorted her to a beautiful room. The peaceful room was all white with big beautiful windows overlooking the Capital. The whole room smelled like flowers because of all the plants that were placed in the room. She was not only impressed with the room but with the staff as well.

The staff was very kind and made her feel at ease. They explained the procedure to her and that there was going to be some discomfort in the hand for a few days. They explained that the pain would go away and she wouldn't even notice the chip. When they placed the chip in her hand it was just a slight pinch but nothing she hadn't experienced before. She had some pretty big wrestling matches with the boys growing up, and some resulted in a few bumps and bruises that were far more painful than this.

The thoughts of growing up in their home and the memories of her family came rushing back to Azalia in that moment. She had tried to forget her memories of back home so she could get on with her life, but these memories proved to be quite persistent. She remembered the hikes and the walks her family used to go on. She remembered the day trips and eating out with her family and friends. She remembered the nights after the Gathering when the family would lay outside under the stars. The family would look up into the heavens dreaming of returning to a normal life one day. She wondered what the family was doing at this very moment. The thought of seeing her brother on the TV came back and she hoped that they were ok.

It took what seemed like forever but the boys had made it across the field and to the walls of the city. After the windmills came crashing down the emergency crews were all over the place. Some were rescuing the officers injured in the chaos and others were trying to repair the fallen structures.

The brothers had decided to take one of the emergency vehicles and make a run for the Capital. They thought that with all the vehicles around that they would be able to drive away unnoticed. The boys saw an opportunity and took it. They crept to the nearest vehicle, climbed in, and began to speed off toward their destination. It seemed like a fool proof plan until they started to drive and realized that non of them had driven before.

They were all over the road and quickly drew attention. One of the officers raised his hands to them as a signal for them to stop.

"Just keep driving Ezra!"

Zavier was shouting at Ezra. Zavier knew that if the brothers stopped their vehicle that there were too many officers to fight. Even for them. The vehicle started to slow as Ezra brought the vehicle to a stop. Apparently Ezra hadn't heard Zavier yelling at him or he was ignoring him. Nether of which was setting right with Zavier.

Ezra had heard Zavier yelling at him but he felt that he could talk his way through this checkpoint. If the boys tried to make a run for the Capital they would never get through the gates. The Capital would be shut down and there would be no way in. Ezra thought to himself that if they could convince this one officer at the checkpoint that they were suppose to be there, and other officers see him let the boys pass, then they should be home free. Smooth sailing to the Capital.

Zaiden could see that his brother was deep in thought. He didn't know what there was to think about. They were not wearing any uniforms and every other person besides them had a uniform with the badge representing the Capital. There was no way that they could talk their way through this. As the boys crept to a halt the officer approached their vehicle. It became clear that Zaiden's fear was being realized.

Zaiden could see the look on the officers face the moment that he recognized that the boys were not wearing uniforms. The officer began to reach for the gun on his hip when Zaiden reached over with his foot and stomped on the gas. The truck came to life and shot forward. Zaiden could see that his brothers were as shocked as the officers when they began to move but he didn't care. He had one goal. They needed past that wall.

Ezra saw the officer reaching for his hip and suddenly the truck sprang forward. Zaiden had stomped on his foot and he would have to remember to give his brother a smack later for that, but for now he knew that he needed to get to that wall in front of them. They needed to get to the wall fast no matter what it took.

The boys were speeding towards the wall and they could hear the bullets pinging off the side of the truck. The windows of the truck were blowing out from the gunfire and glass was flying everywhere. The brothers could see a large number of vehicles following them in the rearview mirror. The were gaining on them. They could see the large gate beginning to move ahead of them. They were closing the gate!

"Can't this thing go any faster? Did you find the slowest truck in the fleet?"

Zavier was a bit panicked. This was not nearly as smooth as what he was hoping it would be. Why couldn't they have got the easy way just this once. Was it so bad if they could have driven through the front gate like other people? His thoughts were interrupted by a loud smash and the truck swinging sideways. The other trucks had caught up and now they were trying to knock the boys off the road.

As the truck swung sideways Zaiden's world slowed as he entered hyperspeed. He had had enough of this. He was looking straight at the driver and passenger of the the vehicle that had pulled beside them. Without a thought he leaped.

He removed his seatbelt and jumped through the window and onto the hood of the other truck that was now firmly planted on the side of theirs. Their windshield was smashed out of the officers vehicle. It was no trouble for Zaiden to slide on the hood, foot extended, and through the gap where the windshield once stood. He made contact with the passenger first. His foot drove the man's head right into the solid brace behind the seat. Zaiden swung his fist and used the back of his hand to strike the driver between the eyes. The driver was dispatched before he even knew what was happening.

The man lost consciences immediately and the truck began to swerve. Zaiden rolled himself back onto the hood and intended to leap toward the window in the boy's truck. The truck Zaiden was on began to twist and started into a roll as he was planting his feet to jump from the truck. Zaiden pushed off as hard as he could but he wasn't going to make it back to the boys vehicle. He was midair and the truck he had just left was now flying effortlessly through the air. The truck was in a full barrel roll. Zaiden reached as far as he could and with one hand gripped the handle of their truck. His world returned to normal speed.

Zavier could feel the truck swing sideways and suddenly Zaiden wasn't in the truck anymore. He looked out his window and could see the two officers suddenly jerk to the side and slump and then their truck went air born. It all happened so fast that he barely registered that his brother was now hanging off the side of their vehicle. Zavier kicked the front door open, grabbed the safety belt with one hand, and leaned out of the moving vehicle to grab his brother.

"Grab my hand with both hands Zaiden!"

Zavier knew that letting go of the handle meant Zaiden would have to trust him to not drop him under the moving truck. Zaiden released his grip on the truck and grabbed on for dear life to his brother.

Zaiden saw the door swing open and his brother hanging out. He heard his instructions but what if Zavier let him go? He could hear the explosion of the rolling truck that was now slightly behind them. It was still close enough to feel the heat from the blast but Zaiden knew it was now or never. He released his grip from the truck and grabbed on with both hands. He hoped that his brother wouldn't drop him.

Zaiden could feel the pavement slicing through his skin as his legs were being dragged from the side of the truck. None of this mission so far would matter if he didn't get back into this truck. He could see that Zavier was pulling with all his might but he didn't have the strength to get him back inside. It was then that Zaiden heard the sound of a nearing truck engine and his world slowed once again as he entered hyper-speed.

Another truck that was filled with officers was now beside the boys as they raced toward the closing gate. It collided with a smash as the boys truck once again jerked sideways. The officers vehicle had hit right where Zaiden had been hanging. Luckily for Zaiden, he heard it just before impact and moved quickly to avoid being crushed. He stepped on the bumper of the vehicle and stepped back into the boys vehicle.

The vehicle struck harder than the last one and Ezra heard the wheel blow out on their truck. How were they going to make it to the gate? How were they going to get through? He took a quick glance in the mirror and saw that the truck that had been trying to force them off the road was now resting in a ditch. That guy would be pretty embarrassed if he knew that he just got out driven by someone who never driven before.

Ezra looked ahead and realized that the gate was almost shut. They were not going to make it. They were not going to be able to get in and save Azalia. That was the last thought before he felt a truck, that seemed to come from no where, collide with his door.

The hit was so vicious that it threw Ezra from the truck and he could hear the vehicle smashing and crumbling as it rolled. He could hear the sound of twisting metal and an explosion. He laid on the ground for a moment to get his bearings. He opened his eyes to see his brothers laying a few feet away. Ezra could hear the sound of gravel crunching under tires and he rolled over and came face to face with the barrel of a gun.

"Looks like your run is over!"

The officer sounded confident but Ezra wondered how confident he would be when he and his brothers got to their feet? Ezra could hear Zaiden groan and he looked in the direction of his brothers. Both brothers were laying in the dirt bloodied and beaten. Ezra looked at Zavier and they locked eyes. He knew that look of determination well. This fight was far from over.

# 14

# How Quickly Things Change

It was when Azalia was walking from the medical centre that she received some of the best news she had ever heard. There was a group of people cheering and clapping as she walked from the room where she received the chip. Treadon was standing with that same smile plastered across his face as he stood arms extended. He pulled her in for a hug. She normally hated being hugged but this seemed different. It was like she was beginning a whole new chapter in her life and this was the initiation.

Treadon allowed everyone to finish their congratulations to Azalia and when they were done he handed her an envelope. Everyone went quiet, still smiling, and with looks of anticipation.

"What is this?"

Azalia figured that it must be something good because everyone looked excited to see what was inside.

"This is your work assignment." Treadon had stepped close and laid his hand on her shoulder.

"We take your personality, passions, and desires. Then we determine if you have the abilities to accomplish your desired occupation. If we feel that it is attainable then we put in motion the training to hone those skills and help you step into your dream job."

It all sounded amazing too Azalia but she wondered if they would really be able to come up with a job that would be her dream job. She wasn't even sure that she knew. As she slipped her fingers into the envelope to pull out the paper, a thought of concern crossed her mind.

"What if I don't like the job that I've been assigned?"

She was turning her head toward Treadon and her eyes rested on his. She could see a slight frustration cross his eyes. It was only for a moment but it was unmistakable.

"It is not about whether you like your job or not Azalia. It is about maintaining order in our society. It is important that everyone knows their place and it is equally important that people do not step outside their role. The government will make sure that you are fed and protected. We will make sure that you are entertained and feel safe but this security comes with an expectation."

Treadon was not even trying to hide his frustration now. It was like a switch was flicked in his mind the moment that Azalia had received this chip.

"We are the ones that will decide where you go and what you do from now on. This chip will help us maintain that order at all cost."

Treadon had lifted Azalia's hand in his as if to drive the point home. She looked at the mark where the chip was now imbedded into her skin and knew that she had made a mistake. This chip was not for her safety as much as it was so she could be tracked like an animal.

"So what happens if I decide that I want to do another job?"

Azalia was afraid to ask. This man that was all smiles a moment earlier was now glaring at her. Not as one who loved her but as one who wanted to control her.

"This is the last time we will have this discussion! I will make this very plain to you. You do not need to worry about whether you like your job or not. You need to worry about doing it well for the betterment of our society."

Treadon had stepped back now and was speaking to Azalia no different than an officer would speak to a rebel. She could feel her heart rate rising and she could feel herself beginning to sweat. For the first time since she had entered the Capital, she felt afraid.

Azalia opened the envelope, still gripped in her hand, and slid the paper out. The word entertainer was written across the top of the page. Underneath were paragraphs outlining her requirements and expectations.

"I don't really sing." Azalia spoke in a quiet whisper. It was so quiet that she barely heard her own voice.

She was not sure how Treadon would react. Would he see this as an act of defiance by questioning the work assignment? Many times in that old abandoned school she had dreamed of living a life with all the modern things she was now surrounded by. In her wildest dreams she didn't think it would be like this.

"You will be given a trainer." Treadon spoke very matter of factly. "You will do your job to our expectations. If you are unable to contribute to our society you will be removed. If you can not contribute to society then you are of no value to us. You have a tremendous opportunity here. If you do well you can travel the world, be famous, and live a life you've always dreamed. If you fail in your role that you've been given then you will be put down like a dog. I expect your full effort in this."

With that statement barely out of his mouth Treadon turned on his heels and headed away from Azalia. He stepped into a crowd of people begging for his attention. Azalia watched as the people scampered to speak with him but she was consumed with the thought that she was going to regret becoming a citizen. What had she done?

Azalia wondered if her family was ok. She wondered if she would ever see them again. She thought about running away from the Capital but they would be able to track her. She thought about not doing her job to show the government that she could not be controlled. She had seen what happens when someone defies the government though and she wasn't willing to face death. She only had one option. Whether she liked it or not, she was going to have to get trained and become an entertainer. Her life literally depended on it.

Azalia sat on a nearby bench, laid her head in her hands and began to weep. As the tears began wetting her cheeks she decided to turn to the only one who could help. She began to pray. She prayed for wisdom and guidance. She prayed for deliverance and hope. Mostly though, she prayed for forgiveness.

Azalia had spent so much time dreaming of living this life only to find out that her old life was far better than she had realized at the time. It seemed like she had been sitting on the bench for an hour when she heard a voice from across the room begin to shout.

"They are coming!!"

She looked up to see the image on the TV screen that was causing such a commotion.. It was a battle raging in the field of windmills that stood just outside the gates of the Capital. On the screen was a young man pushing on a windmill like he was Samson in the temple. The windmill began to tilt and then fall. The windmill began to collide with the windmill next to it and the field of structures all began to fall like dominoes in a hale of explosions. That was when the power went out and the city went dark.

It only took a few moments and the power shot back to life. What Azalia saw on the screen was something that she could not believe. In the midst of the fire and debris stood three young men. Not just any young men but it was her brothers. Azalia knew that her prayer was being answered. They were coming for her.

# 15

# Welcome to the Capital

Ezra laid there with the gun still pointing at his head. He looked past the barrel of the gun and into the eyes of the officer.

"You are going to wish that you never pointed that gun at me. In fact, you all think that you have the upper hand here but my brother's and I are getting through that gate. You have a choice here. You can either let us stand up and walk through that gate or you can fight us. Either way, we will still walk through this gate."

Ezra could feel his heart rate rising and it wasn't because he was scared. He was furious. These officers stood between he and his sister! This gate stood between he and his sister! This government stood between he and his sister! If he had to tear this entire Capital apart he would. He and his brothers were leaving this place with his sister.

Zaiden heard the speech from his brother but he still laid there pretending to be unresponsive. Zaiden chose to lay there and gain a little rest after the truck had flipped and the brothers were thrown out. He could hear the anger in Ezra's voice and he knew that this rest was not going to be long. His eyes fluttered open in time to catch his brother's making eye contact. His attention turned too Zavier and he knew that look well that was plastered on his brother's face. The look on Zavier's face was one of determination. The look wasn't there long before it disappeared. In fact, Zavier disappeared.

Zavier had looked his brother right in the eyes and he knew that his brother was thinking the same thing as him. It was time to end this! His whole world went black and white as he became invisible once again. He could see that his sudden disappearing act startled the officers by the way they shifted their body weight away from where he once stood. Zavier grabbed the officer next to him by the wrist. He rolled him over his shoulder and onto the ground. Zavier threw a quick punch to the throat and the officer was down for good. It all happened so fast that it caught the other officers off guard. Zavier could see that his two brothers didn't take long to catch on to the plan.

Zaiden saw his brother disappear and then the officer that was next to him forced to the ground with a thump. He knew that his brother wasn't thinking this through. There was no plan here. They were going to fight their way out of this and hope for the best.

Zaiden's world slowed as he entered hyper-speed. He stood to his feet and he could see that the officer next to him was shifting his weight to protect himself. It was no use. Zaiden slipped a well placed uppercut onto the officer's chin and sent the man flying. He was still mid air when Zaiden ducked under the levitating body to sweep the legs out from under the next officer. He reached around to grab the foot of the first officer, still hovering in the air, and he swung the officer around colliding the helpless officer with two more of his comrades. All before any of them had realized that Zaiden even moved.

When Ezra saw his brother disappear he knew that it was now or never. He grabbed the barrel of the gun that had been pointing at him and he pulled it toward himself, bringing the officer on the other end with it. Ezra raised his arm and issued a perfectly placed clothesline. The officer fell to the ground without a sound. Ezra grabbed him by the head and picked him up like an NBA player palming a basketball. He hurled the man toward a group of officers that were standing close by. The officer flew through the air like a frisbee and wiped out the group that was standing unsuspecting. They hadn't even seen the soaring body coming. Ezra heard a shot from a gun and felt a searing pain in his shoulder. He had been shot.

Zaiden heard a gun go off and as he looked in the direction of Ezra he could see the blood splatter from a wound. A bullet had hit its mark. The officer who had just shot Ezra was filling the chamber of his gun with another bullet. He wouldn't get the chance to expel it. Zaiden lunged toward him and used the officer's extended arm as leverage as he swung him in a circle. The officer flew threw the air and right into the waiting hand of Ezra.

Ezra felt the searing pain of the bullet. He turn to see where it came from and there was an officer heading straight for him. He reached out and grabbed the man as he was flying through the air. He turned and threw the man straight into the wall. He felt the hands of another officer wrapping around his arms from behind him, but he quickly threw the man over his shoulder and to the ground. Ezra could hear the sound of a drone hovering over head so he grabbed the fallen officer and hurled him toward the drone. The body of the fallen officer hit its mark and knocked it out of the air and to the ground.

Zavier had noticed that in all the commotion there was one of the officers that was not engaging the fight. In fact he looked quite out of place. The officer looked like he was scared to be in the midst of the battle. There was something different about this officer so Zavier made his way over. The officer couldn't tell that he Zavier was standing only inches away staring toward something in the officer's hand. It was some sort of black box that this man was clutching like it was the most important thing in the world. Zavier kicked the back of the officer's knee and forced him to the ground. He grabbed the officer's wrist and pried the devise out of his hand. His world went normal once again as he once again became visible. The officer peered at Zavier terrified that someone could just appear out of thin air like some sort of ghost.

"What is this!"

Zavier was certain it was something important.

"It's nothing! It is a keepsake that I carry to remember my family!" The officer was afraid but Zavier could hear the defiance in his voice.

"If you don't tell me what this is then you will end up like the rest of your buddies! You will all be laying around here like it's midnight at a summer campout."

The officer never said a word. He lifted his thumb to the centre of the devise and applied pressure. Zavier could hear the gate come to life as it began to open. This was their chance to get in.

"Boys! Enough of this! let's get inside!

Ezra could hear a sound from behind him as he heard his brother yell in the midst of the fighting. It never registered right away what was happening until he turned to see what his brother wanted. That was when he could see the gate standing open. The gate was not open the whole way but enough to sneak through the gap. He wasn't sure what Zavier did but he was pretty happy that he did it. Ezra quickly stepped through the open gate.

Ezra stepped out of the chaos and into something he had never seen before. A city so large and bright that it blocked out the stars in the sky. A city so loud with people and advertisements playing on the sides of buildings that they couldn't even hear the war going on outside the walls. He realized in that moment that this was no normal city. He thought to himself that this was a prison. These people thought that they were the ones that were free but really they had isolated themselves into this small space. They could't even see the simple beauty of nature from inside these city walls. His brothers stepped in beside him and they all stared together at their surroundings. They could hear the gate close and they knew that they couldn't just stand where they were any longer. They knew that it was time to move. That was when they heard a siren start to blare. It was so loud that it could be heard over all the noise of the city.

The boys stood in awe as the entire city went silent except for the siren. The adds stopped cycling on the buildings and were replaced by a video of them standing at the gate.

"I guess this means that we are going to have a hard time hiding."

Zaiden was trying to be funny but this was not the time for it. The people and all the cars simply stopped. Every citizen stared at the screen like it was their life line. Suddenly the face of a man that all three boys recognized filled the screen. It was Treadon.

"It seems that there has been a security breach. Do not be afraid Citizens. We would ask that all citizens please return to their homes. The threat will be neutralized momentarily and we will be back to our normal life once again. Let this be a reminder that those who refuse to conform to our way of life are a threat that must be eliminated. We do not intend for this isolation to last long but please do not be upset at your government. We must be diligent to protect our Citizens. We are not the ones causing this issue today. This lockdown is being caused by those who stand by the gate. It is those who have refused to protect mankind. We will take care of this issue and we will all return to normal soon. Thank you for your patience."

Treadon's face fluttered off the screen with his smile still plastered on his face. The boys could see everyone leaving the streets. They thought to themselves that it was strange how quickly a city so full of noise and people, could seem empty in a moment.

The boys could hear the sound of approaching vehicles. The stream of vehicles kept coming and they knew that this was going to be their biggest fight yet. The trucks approached them but then ground to a halt a few hundred feet away. The boys looked at one another and expected the trucks to begin to empty with officers. They were not disappointed.

The brothers watched as the the trucks emptied. There were more officers than the boys had ever seen. They did not know how they were going to be able to defeat this many officers but they knew they were going to have to try. They were determined to leave the Capital with their sister and they would not let anything get in their way.

The officers stood facing the brothers with guns drawn. The boys could hear a strange sound from behind them and turned to see what was happening. Out of the wall slid guns bigger than they had ever seen. The brothers were surrounded on all sides. The guns from the walls were pointed at them as well as hundreds of officers pointing their guns at them. This was not looking to good.

"What are we going to do?" Zaiden whispered to Ezra. He was hoping that there was some sort of plan that Ezra had up his sleeve.

"I don't know."

Ezra was losing confidence for the first time since the brothers had left their parents back in Sussex. Had they come all this way just to be killed at the entrance of the Capital?

The boys were still standing and waiting for someone to make the first move when another vehicle approached the scene. This vehicle was not like the rest of the military vehicles that had now surrounded them. The car that pulled to halt just a few feet away was a luxury car. The door swung open and a man dressed in a sharp suit emerged. He was buttoning his suit jacket as he was stepping out of the vehicles and the boys knew exactly who stood before them. It was Treadon.

Treadon stood facing them for a moment. He let the silence stand between them for what seemed like forever. There was no smile that seemed to be plastered on his face every time you would see him on the TV. He stood silently for a moment peering at them emotionless. Finally he opened his mouth and began to speak to the brothers.

"Did you really think that you were going to walk in to the Capital? Everyone here is fitted with a state of the art chip that will alert us to any suspicious activity. You can't just walk through the front gate without a chip and expect to get far. In fact! You are quite fortunate that those wall cannons did not dismember you the moment you stepped through these gates. So tell me boys, have you come all this way to join the Capital? We could use you guys for some of our military missions."

Ezra was the first to speak.

"We are here for our sister! If you give her to us now we will simply leave." Ezra didn't want to have to fight here. There were too many guns, even for him and his brothers to handle. Treadon allowed a smirk to cross his face before he replied to Ezra.

"You seem to be misunderstanding the situation here. You are not in control. You do not get to decide if there is going to be a fight. You don't get to decide if you are going to leave. You don't even get to decide if you live. The government decides that for you. You are a threat. You carry the virus and by being here you put our population at risk. I should have you put down like a sick dog. I am offering you an option though. You can come to our medical facility and be fitted with a chip. We will determine if you are a carrier of the virus. If you are not a carrier then we will recruit you to our forces. You will all be taken care of and live an enjoyable life. Your other option is to refuse. If this is the option that you choose then we will take you to our holding cells where you will await execution. Seems like an easy choice for me. If you are still trying to decide then let me help a little." Treadon turned to his car and signalled with his hand.

"Bring her to me."

Zaiden could barely stand listening to this man speak. When Treadon signalled to the car Zaiden watched as his sister stepped out. It felt like his heart stopped beating the moment he laid eyes on her. She was dressed better than he had ever seen her dressed. She was barely recognizable. His eyes started to tear up just knowing that she was alright. He could see her eyes welling up with tears as well as she spoke the first words they had heard from her in weeks.

"Hey boys!"

Azalia could hardly get the words out. She was told on the drive over that her brother's lives were in her hands. She was to convince them to become Citizens. If the boys refused to comply then they would be put to death. She knew that they would never choose to become Citizens but she needed to bide some time. She needed to figure out how she was going to save them.

"This place is amazing!" She wasn't sure if she even believed what she was saying.

"We are fed well here and we can play hockey, watch TV, and live our lives unafraid of the world around us. We can live at peace here. Please! Let's just be together as a family. We don't have to live in abandoned buildings any longer. We can live in beautiful homes and have beautiful cars and eat amazing food. We can even travel the world. All you have to do is join the Capital."

Azalia was beginning to weep because she could read the expressions on the boys face. They were not interested in joining the Capital. That was not the only thing she saw though. Azalia could tell by the look on their faces that her brothers felt betrayed, like she had somehow joined the very people trying to destroy them.

"How could you ask us to join these people? You know that we live the way we live and that our family has struggled because of the governments regulations and control!" Zavier was not impressed. They had risked their lives to come all the way here only to find out that Azalia had betrayed them.

"I don't know how you can live with yourself! I will not turn from everything our parents taught us. I will not betray our own parents so that I can have *more things*."

"Enough!" Treadon had heard enough of this conversation.

"Take them! Their choice has been made. We will make an example of them to the people of the Capital. They will be an example of what happens when you rebel against the government!"

Treadon waved his hands toward the officers as he was speaking and the officers approached the boys to cuff them. Ezra began to move toward the officers to defend himself when Zaiden spoke up.

"If we fight here then Azalia may be hurt in the chaos. We can not risk it. Let them take us. God did not bring us all this way to rot in a prison and die for the glory of the government."

The boys took one last look toward their sister as the officers cuffed them and escorted them to a waiting vehicle. Azalia took one glance back as she dipped her head and slid into the back of the car with Treadon. She locked eyes with Zavier one last time as the door closed. The boys were not sure what was going to come next, but this certainly was not going the way they expected.

# 16

# The Ultimatum

The drive back to Treadon's home was quiet. Not one person said a word. Azalia had looked into Zavier's eyes when the car door was closing back at the gate and she could see the hurt and betrayal written on his face. Was this who she wanted to become? Was she willing to have everything she wanted at the cost of her brother's lives? The thoughts haunted her for hours. She had arrived at Treadon's home and walked straight to the guest room without saying a word. She felt empty inside. This did not seem right.

"You are troubled!"

The sound of Treadon's voice startled Azalia and whipped her back to reality.

"Are you second guessing your decision to become a Citizen? Are you missing the life you lived, if that's what you want to call it?" Treadon sounded compassionate but there seemed to be some sarcasm in his words.

"It's not that I want to go back to living the way I used to." Azalia wasn't sure she even believed that anymore.

" I just don't want to lose everyone I love. I want to be able to live here and enjoy this life, but still be able to have my family with me." Azalia knew that this could not be a reality even as the words were escaping her mouth. It didn't stop her, however, from trying to figure out how she could have everything she desired.

"What if you were able to speak to them without all the guns pointing at them? Without all the people and the pressure? Do you think you would be able to convince them to join us?" Treadon could see that there was a deep connection in this family and he was sure that he could use this connection to expose them and get what he wanted. He knew that if the brothers were on his side that there would be no rebellion out there that could stand against his government. He could rid this land of those vermin once and for all.

"I don't understand what you are trying to say?"

Azalia wondered if Treadon was telling her that she could go see her brothers in the holding cell. If she could see them alone then maybe she could convince them that this life is better than how they had been living before. Maybe the government would even allow them to talk to Drew and mom and bring them as well?

"I will give you one hour."

Treadon knew that he needed to limit the time the family would have to speak. The limited time frame would force Azalia to control the conversation. Treadon was betting that if Azalia felt that she was short on time then she would spend that time pleading with her brothers. She wouldn't have enough time with them to be reprogrammed into thinking that the old life was better.

Treadon had weighted his options in his mind and realized that it was worth the risk. If the brothers convinced her to return to their old life then the government would kill them all and there would be 4 less rebels. If she convinced them to become Citizens then he would gain a tremendous asset to becoming unstoppable. It seemed like it was a win for him either way.

Azalia agreed to go meet with her brothers. She was on the drive over when Treadon reminded her that this would be the last time she saw her brothers alive if she couldn't convince them to join the Capital. He wasn't mean about it though. He sounded almost compassionate. He explained to her the threat that those living on the outside posed to the Citizens. He explained that if her brothers did not receive the chip then there would be no way of knowing if they were carrying the virus. If the virus reached the Capital, he explained, there would be many lives lost. If protecting the entire Capital meant removing her three brothers then it was the only compassionate choice to make. Treadon was still imploring Azalia to make her time count when he car pulled up to the building. To Azalia's surprise it was the medical centre.

"Why are we here?" Azalia wondered if there had been a change of plans. "This is where we hold those who refuse to follow the rules." Treadon was speaking as he was opening the door to get out. He turned to Azalia and continued as he reached out his hand to help her out of the car.

"We have a holding cell in the basement. It doesn't need to be large because we have a zero tolerance policy toward rebellion. When someone is caught breaking the rules they are taken here for 48 hours. If the infraction is not severe then there are two possible punishments. They will either have less money placed in their personal account and take a pay cut, or they are reissued another job that is less desirable. For instance, one may go from being an entertainer to being a sewage worker. The individual is given 48 hours to decide if they will take the punishment. If they still refuse to accept their punishment then they will be executed. If their crime is what we determine to be severe, then there will be no option and they will simply be executed."

Azalia was taken back by how straight forward Treadon was speaking about ending a human life. The thought was still bothering her as she and Treadon entered an elevator and descended several floors. The elevator slowed to a stop and the doors slid open to a large room. The room was brightly lit. So bright that Azalia was passed a pair of sunglasses as she stepped out of the elevator. She slipped them on and noticed that everyone in the room was wearing the same glasses except for her three brothers that were sitting in the centre of the room.

In the centre of the room stood a solid shatter proof glass cell. In the cell were three beds and one toilet in the corner. The room was surrounded by officers that were heavily armed and positioned staring straight at the cell. Her brothers looked exhausted. She was sure that they had not slept all night with all this light. Azalia knew that this was a form of torture. They were trying to make the boys so uncomfortable and distressed that they would comply to the government's wishes.

Treadon cleared the room with the wave of his hand. He took one more look at Azalia and stepped onto the elevator once again. Azalia was left alone with her brothers as the doors slid closed. It was the first time she was alone with her family since she was taken. She wasn't sure how to begin.

"What are you doing here?" Azalia spoke the first thing that came to her mind.

"We came here to rescue you!" Azalia could hear the distain in his voice as Ezra spoke. She caught all three of them looking at her hand. They had seen the mark representing the location of the chip and she figured she might as well get it out of the way.

"How was I suppose to know that you were coming? Besides, what is so wrong with what I did? This place has everything. It has good food, entertainment, cars, and I can even travel." Azalia didn't mean to be so harsh with them but it always felt like no one approved of her decisions, and she was tired of it.

"You guys would have made the same choice!"

"No I wouldn't!"

Zavier was shooting back with the same attitude and force that Azalia had started with. Zaiden was not sure why she had even come if she was just here to fight. He spoke up and interrupted his two siblings before this argument got out of hand.

"Why are you here Azalia? We don't need a lecture. We need a plan." Zaiden was certain that they could find a way out of this. He could see the cameras pointing at the cell and recording their every move though. He knew that it wasn't going to be easy.

"A plan?" Azalia said it in a way that made Zaiden feel stupid for even suggesting it.

"You do understand that you guys are not getting out right? The only way you are getting out of here alive is if you join the Capital." Azalia was not interested in waisting her time talking to them about getting out. She knew that she only had a short time to convince them to join the Capital or it was going to be too late.

"What does the Capital have that home doesn't?"

Ezra was speaking calmly to his sister. He was not interested in fighting with her if this was his last time they has to her.

"Really though Azalia. What does this place offer? You get good food? You get to watch TV and listen to music? You get to travel and have things you want? At what cost exactly? You gave up all your freedom for this. They know where you are and what is going on inside your body. They tell you where to work and when to work. They decide your career and how you are going to live your life. How is that a good thing? Not only that, but you are willing to never see our parents again? For what? So you can watch what you want and listen to what you want? You do realize that the government is going to kill us right? The very people that you seem to think is so great because they give you things, is the very group of people that are going to destroy us. Your family!!" Ezra was hoping that he would be able to get through to her, but he wasn't sure it was working at all.

Azalia sat with tears welling up in her eyes. What had she been thinking. All these things that she had been given was nothing more than the government buying her affection. She was giving up her family for what? Ezra had pierced her to the heart with his words. How could she have been so foolish. She knew that she couldn't ask her brothers to join the Capital. She needed to find a way to get her brothers out of this cell and out of the Capital. They spent the remaining time hashing out a plan to escape.

The plan seemed to come together quickly. The siblings knew that they would not be able to escape the cell on their own so they would let the guards do the work. They thought that their moment of escape would happen when the guards transported them from the cell to the room where they would execute them. The plan was that Azalia would ask to view the execution but would sneak out of the room when the boys began their escape. She would use her chip and walk ahead of them causing the automated doors to open. They only needed to get to the main floor and out the main doors. Once they hit the streets they could make a run for it.

The siblings had their plan all hashed out and Azalia approached the cell and placed her hand against the glass. One by one the boys stepped up and placed their hands against cell wall from the opposite side. They only had one shot at this. If this didn't work then it meant that they would all be executed. Azalia was risking her life to break her brothers out of this cell. For the first time in forever she felt like she had a purpose. She was going to save her family.

# 17

## Together at Last

The morning of the execution had arrived and Azalia awoke with the sound of a knock on her door. She crawled out of bed and threw on a bath robe and proceeded to walk across the room. As she opened the door she was greeted by three officers.

"You need to come with us. Mister Treadon has requested your attendance for breakfast." They spoke without emotion and it kind of unnerved Azalia.

"I will be right out. You will need to wait a moment and let me get ready."

Azalia threw a smile on her face as she spoke to the officers at the door but this day was not the kind of day that brought smiles to someone's face. This day was possibly the last time she may ever see her brothers, or anyone, if things didn't work out just right.

Azalia got ready quickly and joined the officers outside her door. They escorted her down a long hall and into a wide open room. The room was furnished with a long table situated in the centre. The table was surrounded by chairs and sitting at the head of the table sat Treadon.

"May I offer you some fresh fruit? It has just arrived this morning. It has arrived straight from Mexico." Treadon barely looked in Azalia's direction as he spoke and she felt like something was a little off about this encounter.

"I did not realize that people still lived in Mexico or that we brought fruit from there." She was trying to make pleasant conversation to keep the mood light. It didn't seem to be working.

"We were not the only nation that had a Gathering. It was a global operation." Treadon was biting into an apple as he peered down the table at Azalia. "The World Organizational League was formed for that very reason.

I am just a player in the game Azalia. I am not the coach." Azalia was beginning to get a bigger picture of the situation. The Government was being run and directed by someone far more powerful.

"That still does't explain why we are having fresh fruit for breakfast." Azalia was trying not to show her distaste for Treadon. She needed to be on his good side if she was going to be able to free her brothers.

"When a Capital is established in a region it is then populated and given a directive. Mexico's Capital has the directive to grow and maintain a fruit harvest for the world. When one is sent to Mexico to become a citizen they must understand that most of the jobs in that region are geared toward feeding the world. There are ten Capitals set up around the world and each have their own purpose."

Treadon was speaking but Azalia had the escape running through her mind. She hd no interest in hearing this conversation but she sat silently and allowed Treadon to continue on.

"The Capital in China focused on technical advancement and we have a focus on resources. We supply the world with oil and water. We also supply them with gold and silver. You name it and we work to produce it. The world is a much different place than it was before the Gathering. We work together now. If you do not want to work in unity with all mankind then you are of no use. This brings us to why you are here." Treadon set his apple down and leaned toward Azalia.

"Why have your brothers decided not to join us?"

Azalia was afraid that this conversation was going to cost her the chance to get close to her brothers. She knew that she needed to say whatever was necessary to stay on Treadon's good side.

"I spoke with them but they are brainwashed into thinking that we are still the enemy. They do not understand that what we are creating is necessary for mankind's survival." The words almost sounded convincing coming from her mouth but just saying the words made Azalia want to vomit.

"I apologize for failing you sir." Those words made Azalia's skin crawl even as she spoke them. She wanted this breakfast to end so she could be out of this man's presence. Treadon softened his posture and leaded back on his chair.

"Would you like to say goodbye to them?"

Azalia was startled at the request but how could she pass up the opportunity to speak to them one last time. She worked up some tears in her eyes and replied.

"You would do that for me? How can I ever thank you?" Azalia hoped that she wasn't over selling it.

"Come! Let us see your brothers one last time."

Treadon stood from the table and started toward the door. Azalia jumped from her seat and followed behind.

Azalia and Treadon arrived at the medical facility and the place was buzzing with life. Everyone was just going about their business like it was just another day. Meanwhile, on the drive to the facility every screen was playing the scene of her brothers standing at the gate surrounded by the officers. Under the scene on the screen the words "The traitors die today" was scrolling across the bottom. When she was passing through the lobby of the medical building the volume was just high enough on the TV to hear the commentators speaking about the threat that these 3 boys posed. The commentators were commenting that it was a win for all mankind that this threat was being eliminated. It was like the media repeated the same message over and over to brainwash the people into believing what the government wanted them to believe.

Azalia could not help but feel a pity for these people living in the Capital. They had been convinced by the government that everyone outside the city was a threat. The government had convinced the people to the point that Citizens were able to go on with life, while people were being murdered in the basement of the very building they were working in. If turning a blind eye to murder was not bad enough, the Citizens actually agreed with government's approach. The whole thought of it unnerved Azalia.

Azalia had desired more than anything to be part of their world. Now she was a Citizen but she could see through the fresh fruit, the new cars, the beautiful homes, and the entertaining lifestyle. She could see that behind it was something far more sinister. The government controlled their entire lives. They were told what to think, where to work, and where they could travel. The Citizens were under constant surveillance by the government. The part that bothered Azalia the most was that the Citizens actually thought they were the free ones. The Citizens had been convinced that those outside the walls of the Capital were the ones that were suffering.

Azalia and Treadon stepped into the elevator. Treadon pushed the button and the doors began to slide shut. Azalia took one more glance into the lobby as the doors came together and was hit again by the reality of the situation. Her life was about to change forever and these people were going to cheer. They were going to rejoice at the death of her brothers, or so they thought. As she could feel the elevator began to move she wondered if her brothers were prepared for the great escape?

When the doors opened Azalia was startled by what she saw. There were so many officers that she could hardly move through them all.

"What is going on?"

Azalia looked into the direction of Treadon when she spoke. He gazed at her and spoke without a drop of emotion.

"There have been multiple reports that these brothers of yours were able to achieve superhuman abilities on the field. We are simply taking precautions to make sure that this day goes as planned."

"What do you mean by 'superhuman abilities?'"

Azalia knew that her family had trained for years in order to learn to fight because Drew was convinced that the government would come for his family one day. She felt kind of bad for giving him such a hard time about it now but this still seemed a bit excessive.

"So am I going to be able to see my brothers or not?"

Azalia could feel their plan unraveling before her very eyes.

Treadon motioned toward the cell in the centre of the room and the bodies of the officers parted like the red sea. At the end of the tunnel of bodies stood the cell with the brothers standing by the door. Azalia approached the cell and placed her hands on the glass wall. Ezra stepped forward and placed his hands against hers. As she peered into his eyes she was struck by the look. It was not one of defeat but rather one of determination. She realized that the boys still planned on getting out, but how?

"Open the cell door!" Treadon spoke with a determination and force in his voice.

"You had one use for us Azalia, and that was to convince your brothers to become Citizens. You failed in such a simple task. Our society has little use of someone like you that will fail in something so simple."

The words pierced Azalia to the core. She was surprised how much the words of rejection hurt even from someone she didn't even like, or trust. She felt hands being placed on her back and they were forcing her into the cell. She struggled against the officer but it was no use. The tears streamed down her face as she began to scream. She knew that this meant she was going to be executed with her brothers. How she wished she could just be back with her family and live in an abandoned school in an abandoned town. How she missed her simple life.

Azalia felt one final shove from the officer as she fell through the cell door. She fell to the ground and turned to look helplessly at the door. Treadon stood on the other side of the door staring emotionless at her.

"Let us rid this world of these vermin."

Treadon turned his back to walk away, motioning with his hands to shut the door. An officer stepped forward and swung the door closed. Only, the door didn't fully close. The officer looked down to see Ezra's foot holding the door open. He looked straight into the eyes of Ezra as a smirk emerged on Ezra's face.

"Let's do this."

Zaiden watched as the officer threw his sister to the ground. He had seen enough. The officer had tried to shut the door on Ezra's foot and he heard Ezra say something in return but he wasn't sure what Ezra said. What Zaiden could see though was the fear in the officer's eyes. Zaiden knew this was the moment they had been waiting for. His world slowed as he entered hyper-speed and he saw Ezra lift his foot and kick the cell door with so much force that it flew off its hinges. The door flipped end over end through the air striking the front row of officers. The door was still in the air when Zaiden exited the cell.

Zaiden launched through the air and planted his knees into the chest of the first soldier he came to. He used the officer's body like a spring board and lunged at the next officer beside him. His fist collided with the next officer but he didn't stop there. He round house kicked and took out another two soldiers. He glanced back toward the cell that was now empty and he could see officers falling to the ground all around the room.

Zavier was standing beside Zaiden when he took off. It was that moment when his world went black and white as he became invisible. He walked out of the cell and stepped over the bodies of the officers that had been subdued by Zaiden. Zavier looked across the room and could see Treadon and began walking straight toward him.

Treadon was almost to the elevator and had himself surrounded by officers. They didn't even see Zavier coming. He grabbed the first officer, wrapped his arm around his neck, and flipped him over his shoulder. The officer landed with a thump. Zavier stood from his crouch and planted an uppercut firmly on the chin of the next officer. He could see the face of Treadon and it was one of terror. Zavier stepped forward now only inches from the terrified Treadon's face.

"Boo!"

Treadon jumped back firmly against the elevator doors.

"How is this possible?" Treadon's voice didn't sound so confident now.

The officers standing on either side of Treadon had heard the voice as well and raised their guns. Zavier grabbed their heads and pulled them together, knocking them both out. Zavier's world went back to normal as he became visible once again. He wanted Treadon to see the one who was going to bring him down.

"This is over!"

Zavier was lifting his fist when he heard a scream. He turned to see an officer dragging his sister with a gun pointing at her head.

"Not yet it's not."

Zavier looked back to Treadon and his smile had returned to his face.

"You think you can beat me? If you beat me there will be another. I will simply be replaced and who ever is next will be coming after you. You and your family of misfits will not survive this." Treadon's confidence was returning in his voice.

"You come to us with guns, an army, and fear. But we come with the spirit of God all mighty." With those words, Zavier's world went black and white as he once again became invisible.

Zavier leapt into the air, spun around, and kicked Treadon. He didn't see it coming and collapsed to the floor. Zavier looked back toward his sister and he could see several officers laying around her and Ezra standing above her. Zavier knew that Ezra must have taken care of it.

Ezra had kicked the door with enough force to knock it off its hinges. He knew that the fight was on the moment the door came off and collided with the first officers. There was no turning back now. He stepped out of the cell, grabbed the gun of the first officer, and ripped it from his grip. He swung the gun like a baseball bat and knocked out three officers before they could register in their mind what was happening. He kneeled down and grabbed the ankle of one of the fallen officers, swung him around, and took the feet out from underneath several other soldiers that were standing on guard. They all fell in a heap and groaned from the pain. He heard a scream from behind him and noticed an officer dragging Azalia.

Ezra picked up a body of a fallen officer and tossed it like a child would throw their toys. The body soared across the room and into the officer dragging Azalia. Azalia looked toward Ezra and he could see the fright and confusion. He ran to her and extended his hand.

"Come on, we have to go. We can't just sit here." Ezra didn't mean to sound rude but he needed her on her feet so they could get out. It was only going to be a matter of time before more officers arrived.

"How is this possible?" Azalia was terrified and Ezra knew it.

"We will explain later but for now here is the short version. We prayed that God would help us save you. So we woke up with these abilities. I'm sure that someone will write down this story at some point and you can read it then. Now can we just go?"

Ezra extended his hand and this time Azalia took it. He pulled her to her feet and turned toward the elevator. Three officers stood between him and the door to freedom but Ezra knew that it was going to take more than that.

"You want some? Let's see how this is going to work out for you."

Ezra was pretty confident that this was going to be easy. He took his first step toward them when suddenly one officer's gun flew into the air, his legs now over his head, and he was landing on the floor. The officer was barely hitting the ground when the officers beside him collided heads so hard that it sounded like someone was cracking an egg. They fell in a heap and suddenly Zaiden was standing on his defeated foes.

"You ready to get out of here?" Zaiden was panting heavily but the smile on his face said that he was actually enjoying this. The siblings met in the elevator and began the ascent to the ground floor.

"BING!"

The elevator signalled that they had arrived on the ground floor. They just needed to get out the front doors and they would be home free. The doors swung open but between the siblings and the front door stood multiple officers. These officers looked like they had been waiting for their arrival. The door wasn't even fully open and Zavier and Zaiden were gone. Ezra stepped out of the elevator with Azalia in tow and began his path to the front door.

The doors were not even fully open and Zaiden knew what he must do. He needed to clear a path for escape. His whole world slowed as he entered hyper-speed and he could see officers standing on nearby stairs with their guns drawn. He ran faster than he had ever ran yet. He ran so fast that he was able to run on the wall like he was running across the floor. He started up the stairs and close lined the first officer. The first officer hadn't even hit the ground and Zaiden was wrapping his arm around the neck of the second. He used his momentum and swung the officer around, hitting the third officer and knocked them both over the ledge. Zaiden could hear their screams and then a thump. He continued to the stair case coming down the other side of the room but he was aware that he running out of time. He was reaching the first officer when he heard the first shot fire from a gun.

Zavier saw Zaiden lunge toward the door and then he was gone. Zavier's world went black and white as he became invisible. He headed straight for the secretary. He knew that if she was able to call out on her phone then more reinforcements would arrive shortly. That might be even too much for the brothers to handle even with their gifts. He arrived at her desk and watched as she slipped to the ground to not be seen. She was starting to dial and Zavier kneeled beside her then reappeared out of thin air. The lady shrieked with fright.

"Don't be afraid. We are not going to hurt you. I just can't allow you to call."

Zavier grabbed the cord with his hand and pulled so hard that it pulled the cord right out of the wall. He laid it beside the frightened lady and smiled at her.

"Enjoy the show and stay low." He gave her a wink and suddenly disappeared before her eyes.

Zavier leapt over the desk and planted a firm kick to the sternum of an unsuspecting officer. There was another officer standing next to him with his gun pointing straight toward the elevator door. It was that moment when Zavier heard the shots and saw the flash of light coming from the barrel of the gun.

Ezra stepped out of the doors with Azalia dragging behind him.

"Stay behind me! This could get a bit messy."

Ezra barely made it out the door and he was met with the butt end of a gun. It hardly phased him. He grabbed the officer by the arm and threw him toward the doors. The body hit two more officers that were standing between the siblings and their destination. Ezra grabbed a nearby officer and pulled the stunned man toward himself. He summersaulted over him, held on to the officer's head, and slammed him to the ground. Ezra turned toward the door and gripped Azalia's hand tight as he continued to pull her along. That was when the shots started to fill the room.

Ezra pulled Azalia close and wrapped his arms around her to shield her from the gun fire. He could feel the bullets hitting him and he could feel the searing pain, but he knew that he needed to get her out of the building. He pulled Azalia with him as they crashed through the front door and onto hot pavement awaiting them outside. He looked up from the ground and saw a car parked with the driver staring in unbelief. Ezra shoved Azalia toward the car.

"Get in!! I need to get the boys!"

Azalia heard the gun fire and Ezra immediately pulled her toward him. She could hear the bullets hitting the floor all around them and was wondering how was this possible that they were not getting hit? She felt herself lifted from the ground and was suddenly flying through the front door with her brother. She heard him tell her to get in the car but he shoved her so hard that she couldn't have stopped if she tried. He turned to go back in after their brothers and that was when Azalia noticed the blood. He had been shot! How was he still alive? How was he still fighting?

Zaiden heard the first shot go off and and he saw the bullets flying toward Ezra. Zaiden continued down the stairs and took out the remaining two officers. The first officer with a well placed punch but the second he planted his fist into the officer's elbow. That drove the barrel of the gun that the officer was holding into the air and away from his siblings. Zaiden spun around to the front of the unsuspecting officer and pushed the gun into his face. The officer dropped to the ground and left Zaiden holding the gun.

Zaiden spun around, gun in hand, toward the officers that littered the building's lobby. He pulled the trigger and the gun vibrated in his hands as the bullets filled the air. He had no intention of hitting any officers, he just fired over their heads causing them to run for cover and buy his family enough time to escape. Zaiver suddenly appeared in the middle of the room in the midst of the hail of gunfire.

"Run!! I will catch up!"

Zaiden hoped that his brother wouldn't argue and he didn't. They made eye contact for a moment and Zavier was gone once again.

Zavier had herd the first shot go off and he ran straight toward the officer beside him. He grabbed the gun with one hand, and with his other arm planted his elbow in the neck of the officer. When the officer hit the ground the bullets began to fly. Zavier looked toward the staircase and could see his brother filling the air with bullets but he noticed that he wasn't hitting a soul. Either he was a really bad shot or he was doing this on purpose. Zavier's world went back to normal and he became visible so that his brother could see him. He could hear Zaiden shout to get out so he took one last look up and disappeared.

Zavier was heading out the door when he met Ezra making his way back in. He could see that his brother had been shot yet he was still heading back in for them! Zavier reappeared in front of Ezra and stopped him before he could reenter the building.

"Zaiden has got this. We need to get you to the car and we need to get out of here. Zaiden will catch up." Ezra took one last look toward the building but climbed into the back of the car reluctantly.

"Let's go! We are heading toward the gate!" Azalia was shouting at the driver.

"If I drive you to the gate then the government will kill me!" The driver was in a bad situation and Ezra knew it.

"Get out, I'm driving!"

Ezra shoved the driver out the door, climbed over the seat, grabbed the wheel, and planted his foot to the floor. They were almost out. This was almost over. Suddenly the passenger door flew open and Zaiden was sitting beside him.

"Who let him drive? Last time he drove he flipped the car." For the first time in a long time the family shared a laugh. They were feeling like they had made it. They were really going to get out of the Capital. It was then that the car lurched sideways, and was accompanied by the sound of scraping metal. The officers were not going to let them out that easy. It looked like they were going to need to fight their way out of the Capital. The boys wouldn't have it any other way.

# 18

# The Great Escape

"You've been shot!!" Azalia didn't care who was driving the car but she did care that her brother wasn't going to die in the front seat.

"Get his shirt off so we can see how bad it is!"

Zaiden was helping to pull off Ezra's shirt and the car lurched sideways again. The government was not going to let them escape the Capital.

"Just keep driving Ezra and don't let them stop us! We need to buy some time to get you patched up somehow."

Azalia was still speaking but Ezra could hardly hear her. It was like he couldn't even feel the pain anymore. He thought that his body must have gone numb from the pain or he was slipping into shock. Either way there seemed to be more important things right now than trying to get him patched up.

"I'm fine! Let's just get out of this place. What way do we go Azalia? You've been here longer then us."

Ezra took a sharp left turn as he spoke sending Zaiden colliding with the passenger door. Zaiden almost had Ezra's shirt off and even Ezra noticed that there seemed to be a lot of blood. He looked in the rearview mirror and noticed the other cars swerving on the road behind him. They were still hot on his tail.

"Uh guys?"

Zaiden was staring at his brothers bloodied body and he sounded confused as he spoke.

The other siblings leaned forward from the back seat to get a better look and what they saw caused a confused look to cross their faces as well. They could see that Ezra was riddled with bullet holes. They didn't take the time to count but there must have been fifteen of them. It was impossible that Ezra was still alive let alone moving. As impossible as it was that Ezra was still alive, what really had the siblings staring with their mouths gapped open was the fact that the bullets were all visible just below the surface. In fact, some of them were falling back out of the holes that they had created.

"What are you staring at?" Ezra was still trying to concentrate on the road but he couldn't ignore the looks of his siblings.

"Well I think you are going to be fine." Azalia wasn't sure what was going on but she knew her brother was going to be okay. They had bigger problems now.

"Just get us out of this place and let's get home."

Azalia was directing Ezra down one street after another but it was like the government knew every move they were making. It seemed like the government knew what they were going to do before they even made a move.

The siblings car drifted around a corner and was met with a bone crushing hit. The car swerved a few times and Ezra wasn't able to keep it under control. Their car careened toward a line of parked vehicles and Ezra saw that some people were climbing out of one of the cars, unsuspecting of the carnage that was approaching them. Ezra began to honk the horn frantically trying to get the people to move. Just before the siblings collided with the parked car the people leapt in every direction to avoid being killed by the speeding vehicle.

The sound of the accident was deafening. The sound of glass shattering and the noise of crunching metal echoed down the street. Debris from the accident was scattered all over the road as the car ground to a halt on its roof. The siblings crawled out of the wreckage as the government pulled to a stop and surrounded them. They were closed in on all sides. This was the moment that the boys knew would come. It was time to stop running and it was time to fight their way out.

Zaiden was the first to move. The officers were still exiting their vehicles when Zaiden exited the wrecked car and ran straight toward them. He kicked the door shut on the first vehicle as the officer was still exiting. Zaiden could hear the sheik from the officer as his arm remained trapped inside the vehicle with the rest of his body standing on the outside. Zaiden pushed off from the closed door and slid across the roof of the vehicle next to him. The officer was sliding out of the passengers side and Zaiden's foot connected with his head. Zaiden landed on the ground beside the fallen officer and looked back toward his family. Ezra had already joined the fight.

Ezra was still gripping the steering wheel tight in his hands when he looked across the wrecked car toward Zaiden. He watched as his brother jerked forward in his seat and then he was gone. He could see the bodies of officers dropping on the street and he knew that the fight was on.

He reached around and grabbed the door from their car and with one quick tug he ripped the door right off its hinges. He spun around and launched the door toward the officers who had now exited their vehicles. The door struck four of them head high and sent them cartwheeling. Ezra ran to the closest government vehicle and began to lift on the front end. He could hear the springs making noise and then the sound of the back bumper scrapping the pavement. He had lifted the front end of the car over his head. He tossed the car sideways and rolled it on top of the car next to them. He looked back toward Azalia and Zavier. Only Azalia was standing there. Zavier had joined the fight.

Zavier didn't hesitate. The moment Zaiden made his move Zavier's world went black and white as he became invisible. He could see the glowing bodies of his adversaries and it was bad. Really bad.

As far as Zavier could see he saw the glow of bodies coming their way from every direction. How were they ever going to get out of this alive. He looked across the street and could see an alley way a short distance away. That was their ticket to freedom. If they made the officers fight them in a smaller space, the siblings would only have to fight a few officers at a time. There was no way that the officers would be able to surround them. The problem was the crowd of officers that stood between the family and the alley.

An officer was heading straight toward Zavier and Azalia but he knew that the officer couldn't see him. Zavier reached out, grabbed the barrel of the gun, and pushed it away from the direction of his sister. He crouched down, spun round and swept the feet from underneath the advancing officer. Zavier pointed the gun that was still in his hand toward the alley way. He pulled the trigger and felt the gun shaking in his hands. The bullets were flying in every direction.

"This thing is a lot harder to aim than I thought." Zavier was speaking but he was sure that no one could hear him. The sound of gunfire was deafening.

Officers were running in every direction. They had no idea where the next bullet was headed and neither did Zavier for that matter. His plan worked though. The officers were running for dear life and in the process they had made a pathway toward the alley.

"Come on!" Zavier yelled toward his siblings as he once again appeared out of nowhere.

The family ran toward the alley. Once Zavier had fired off the first round of bullets toward the officers, the air was being littered with gunfire. The siblings could see puffs of dust and the brick from the buildings chipping and breaking away as they ran. The bullets were missing their mark, but barely. They ran down the short alley and onto the next street. They looked up to the building across from them and on the building was a large screen live streaming their entire escape.

"How is his even possible? It's like they know every movement we are making."

Zaiden was getting frustrated. It was one thing to fight their way out but he didn't intend on fighting the entire government forces.

"It's me!" Azalia lifted her hand as she spoke.

"They can monitor my every move. They know when my heart rate drops slightly so they would be able to tell if we felt safer. They would know that we were in hiding and exactly where because of the tracking capabilities of this chip. We have to get this thing out. If I still have this in me when we leave the Capital they will be able to follow us all the way back home. We can't put mom and Drew at risk. We have to get this thing out."

Zaiden looked to the street and he could see officers driving straight toward them. He looked behind him and could see officers entering the alley from the other end as well. They needed a plan and they needed to do something now.

Zaiden entered hyper-speed and ran across the street to a parked car. He drove his elbow through the side window and grabbed a piece of glass before it even had time to fall to the seat. He pivoted on his heels and headed straight toward Azalia. She still had her hand extended still talking about the chip in her hand. He extended his arm, glass in hand, and sliced into her skin. It was happening so fast that Zaiden hoped that the whole thing would be over before Azalia even realized anything was happening.

The First slice exposed the chip but it didn't just drop out like Zaiden hoped. Tiny little wires had attached themselves to the bone and nerves but he didn't have time to worry about how to take this thing out delicately. The chip needed to come out. He reached into her hand with two of his fingers and pulled. His finger slipped on the chip that was coated with blood so he used the glass once more. He used the glass and peeled the chip off her bone. He could tell that Azalia was starting to pull her hand back but he was finished. Zaiden's world went back to normal speed once again.

"Ahhhhhhhh, They shot my hand!!"

Azalia was screaming as she looked down toward her hand. It was bleeding and there was a gapping whole from where her chip used to be. She looked toward Zaiden and he was standing with a bloody piece of glass in one hand and a computer chip in the other.

"Are you insane?" Azalia was not thinking about the chip being out of her hand. She was far more concerned with the fact that her brother just cut her with glass.

"Took care of the problem didn't I?" Zaiden smiled as he spoke.

"Guys!"

Zavier was not interested in hearing his siblings bicker. He was more concerned with how they were going to get out of this Capital.

"What direction do we go Azalia?"

"That way!"

Azalia spoke as she pointed down the street. Even as she spoke he could feel her heart thumping out of her chest. Her finger was not only pointing in the direction of the gate but it was also pointing straight toward an oncoming army of officers.

"Well I guess we know where we are heading then." Ezra spoke as he stepped up beside Azalia.

"I didn't come all this way to just give up now."

The words hardly escaped Ezra's lips when the family heard a loud bang. They could see smoke beginning to rise from the gate that stood at a great distance down the street. The officers that stood between the siblings and the gate turned to look behind them. Again, there was another loud bang and this time the siblings could see fire. There was one more loud bang and the gates swung open. As the gates parted the siblings could see Auston and Mitchell emerge from the smoke billowing from the explosions at the gate. Not only the brothers but an entire army of resistance fighters.

"The odds just became more even." Ezra spoke as he began to run toward the officers trapped in the middle.

It was time to end this.

# 19

# The Fight for Freedom

There were bullets flying everywhere. Azalia crouched behind a nearby car as she heard people on the streets screaming and running. She looked towards a building, fitted with a large TV screen. On the screen was a bird's eye view of the battle going on in front of her. As she looked to the sky, she, could see drones flying everywhere.

"The officers have an advantage!" Azalia was looking at Zavier, who had followed her behind the car.

"We have to figure out how to take that advantage away!" Azalia knew that if this battle lasted too long, the World Organizational League would catch wind of the battle and send troops. With the whole world sending in troops, even her brothers couldn't continue the fight.

It didn't take long before Zavier had a plan. His whole world went black and white and he was once again invisible. With people running in every direction and chaos everywhere, if he were honest, he kind of liked the adrenaline this type of mayhem brought. He ran across the street, into a store, and made his way to the counter looking for a lighter. He quickly found one and leapt toward the tiny orange object, grabbing it and made his way back towards Azalia. He was half- way across the street when he saw an officer attempting to pull his sister out from behind the car. The officer had no idea that Zavier was standing right beside him. Zavier kicked the back of the officer's leg and they buckled under the force of the impact. He quickly fell to his knees. Zavier spun around, with all the force he could muster, and connected the back of his fist with the officer's face. It all happened so fast that the officer didn't have time to react. He was standing one second and lying motionless on the ground the next. Zavier's world went back to normal and he was once again visible. He handed Azalia the lighter.

"I have a plan."

Azalia didn't think she would ever get used to Zavier just appearing out of nowhere, but she was grateful for his help. He handed her the lighter and filled her in with his plan. He was going to go down the street and join the fight but she had an important mission. She needed to start lighting the shops, the cars and anything else that would burn, on fire. The smoke would go up in the air which would begin to block the view from the drones.This would put the resistance and the officers on more of a level playing field. Zavier was insistent that he show her exactly what he wanted her to do, but Azalia was pretty confident that Zavier just liked to light things on fire. After he had lit a couple of stores, he smiled then vanished. Azalia looked toward the battle hoping that her brothers would be okay. Ezra had seen the gate swing open and he knew that this was the moment they were looking for. The officers surrounded, them and it was the advantage the brothers needed. Ezra ran straight toward the officers, and as he reached the first officer, Ezra flicked him aside like a bug. The officer flew through the air and into a nearby car. The next officer turned and took a swing at Ezra. Ezra ducked under the punch and came up with an uppercut, sending the officer tumbling through the air. Ezra barely landed the punch when he could see another punch coming from out of the corner of his eye. Quickly lifting his hand to block it, he countered the officer's punch with a blow of his own, right into the officer's sternum. The officer flew into a parked vehicle and slumped to the ground. Ezra was suddenly surrounded by officers and with every swing of the officer's fists, Ezra countered. While officers fell, one right after the other, Ezra took a quick glance towards the gate and saw the resistance pinned down. Officers were firing an endless barrage of bullets towards the group when Ezra headed over to his friends to help. Noticing Zaiden was working his way towards the officers, Ezra knew that it would not go well for the officers.

Zaiden saw the gates swing open and he knew that this was going to be their best chance at escape. His world then seemed to slow down while he shot off like a cannon.

He ran as fast as he could straight towards the resistance and was already to the officers when they lifted their guns to fire. He looked towards the resistance and realized that they were still coming through the gates. They would be mowed down with gun fire. Zaiden changed his course and headed straight towards the officers on the front line. He reached the first one and grabbed his gun with one hand, swung low with his fist, and took his legs right out from underneath him. Zaiden leapt over the body as it was falling, and body checked the next officer. The officer went flying into the other officers standing by him. Their guns went off, but now they were pointing up in the air. But, Zaiden didn't stop there.

Noticing officer's getting out of the vehicle next to him, he kicked the door shut sending the officer back into the vehicle. Zaiden rolled over the hood of the vehicle and landed a firm punch to the temple of another officer. Zaiden had arrived just in time, as the officer was raising his gun toward the resistance.

Zaiden was moving so fast that the resistance couldn't even see him as bullets began to riddle the street. Zaiden slid under the nearest car and his world returned to a normal speed. The sound of bullets pinging off the car was deafening and the ground was being chipped away as the projectiles missed their mark. Zaiden shuffled his way towards the back of the car to take better cover. As he slid himself out of the back of the car he rose up, right between two officers. They were startled as much as he was. The first officer threw a punch but Zaiden caught it. The second officer spun around and attempted to land a knee into Zaiden's gut but Zaiden lifted his own knee and blocked the blow. He then brought down his lifted knee and planted his heel on the toes of the second officer. Leaning towards the first office, Zaiden landed a firm elbow to the neck. Then he turned with all the force he could muster and landed a perfectly placed punch to the jaw of the second officer, sending him to the ground. Zaiden turned to the first officer again and grabbed his head with both hands. Leaping into the air and using the officers head as leverage, planted his knee into his forehead. The officer dropped like Goliath on an Israeli battlefield. Zaiden turned toward the gate once again, and through the smoke billowing down the street, could see the resistance standing in the gate with arms extended. Zaiden wanted to run to them and just get out of the Capital, but he needed to make sure that there was no sibling left behind this time.

Azalia had done what she was supposed to do. She had lit the fires and now the air was filled with a thick smoke. There was no way that the Government could see what was going on. She could hear the gunfire down the street but the sound of engines roaring, and an army marching, grabbed her attention. As the smoke billowed by her she could see an army of officers approaching. They needed to get out of the Capital now! Turning and running towards the gate, Azalia was about halfway there when she heard the sound of Zavier calling her name.

"Azalia! What are you doing? You are going to get yourself killed!" Zavier was standing over a body of a fallen officer, which he had just subdued.

"Find somewhere to hide, and we will get you when this is over."

Azalia knew that her brother meant well, but he had no idea what she saw coming down the street. "You need to follow me. We need to get out of the capital now!! There is a bigger army than I've ever seen and they are just down the street. Come on!!" Azalia was still running but she was waving at Zavier to follow her. Zavier must have heard the panic in her voice, or saw the fear in her eyes, because he didn't argue, but immediately followed her.

There was a break in the smoke as the two siblings arrived at the battle by the gate. Azalia ran right into Zaiden. Spinning her around, he slid her feet from under her. As she was falling backwards, she saw a foot narrowly missing her face. An officer had been standing in the smoke and attempted to take her out. Zaiden flipped backwards over the officer and stood behind him. The officer turned and was met with a fist full of knuckles.

"There are more officers coming. More than I've ever seen!"

Azalia was in panic mode. Her brothers obviously knew how to fight but she knew when it was time to run. And now was the time. The three siblings ran between the vehicles and right to the space between the gate and the officers. Ezra stood there still heaving, and almost out of breath. Under his feet were several officers who thought they could match him. They were wrong. Azalia explained to Ezra and the resistance that they were out of time. It was now or never. They needed to exit the gate and get to freedom. They would not survive the coming enemy.

The resistance slipped back out of the gate, and the siblings were on their way out, when the first bullet narrowly missed them. First there was one ping, then another, and then so many that the sound meshed into a jumbled mass of noise. Their time was up. The army had arrived. Azalia slipped through the gate and reached her hand back. Zavier was the next through and Zaiden was right behind him. Ezra was only about half-way through the gap when he stopped.

"If we don't close the gate, they are just going to follow us through. We have to cross the field of windmills but we'll be sitting ducks if they follow us through!"

Ezra spoke with an urgency that the siblings were not used to hearing from their brother. He took one last look at his siblings and turned towards the gate. Grabbing both doors, one in each hand, he began to pull his arms together, but they didn't budge.

Zaiden could see the sparks from the bullets narrowly missing his brother. It wasn't going to take long before the bullets met their mark.

"Come on Ezra! We can just run. We will be ok. We just need to get out of here now!!" Zaiden was yelling at his brother. He couldn't understand why he wouldn't just listen.

"If you don't come now, none of us will make it out of this alive! Would you just come!" Azalia was desperate now. She knew that her brothers could fight, and they might be able to get out of a few jams, but getting out of this situation now was impossible. They needed to leave now!

"If you don't stop, I'm leaving!"

Zavier had had enough of this. Did he like beating people up? Sure, he did! Did he like setting things on fire? Sure, he did! Did he like getting shot at? Nope! Did he like seeing his family in danger? Nope! But, it was time to leave and he couldn't understand why his brother wouldn't just come. The thought was hardly entering his mind when he saw the first bullet hit its mark.

It had hit Ezra's leg and his body buckled. He knew that he couldn't give up though. If the army got through the gate, it was all over. He began to pull even harder and swore he felt the gate move. It was then that the second bullet hit another mark. A searing pain shot through his arm. Another one hit his leg, then another one into his shoulder. He knew that he had to ignore the pain and, just then, felt the gate beginning to move. Ezra looked to his side and there stood Azalia.

"We are not leaving without you."

She leaned her shoulder into the gate and pushed. Beyond Azalia stood Zavier who was pushing with all his might. On Ezra's other side stood Zaiden. They had all come together to push. The thought of the siblings all working together gave Ezra the extra strength he needed. Ezra pushed harder than he had ever pushed before and suddenly the gate moved.

At first the gate seemed like it was barely moving but then it began to move faster and faster until it was finally shut. There was some broken down vehicles from the last battle, so Ezra pushed them in front of the gate to secure it. They could hear the army on the other side trying to get through but it was going to take them a little while. The siblings knew that it would buy them enough time to escape. They took one last look at the capital and started their long journey home.

Ezra laid his arms over his brothers, one on each side. As they began to carry him, he could feel the bullets, that had riddled his body, fall from his open wounds. They were finally back together and they were looking forward to a nice quiet life once again. They walked quietly across the field of windmills before Zavier finally spoke.

"Well, that could have been easier."

# 20

# No Place Like Home

The siblings travelled with the resistance until they reached the ruins of Montreal. It had only taken a few hours after the group left the Capital and they could hear the familiar sound of the drones over head. They didn't know how long it would take for the government to repair the gate but they figured that defending the Capital was going to be more important to the government then tracking them all down. Once the Capital was repaired then the resistance and siblings both were sure that the government would be coming for them.

The siblings tried to convince Auston and Mitchell to leave Montreal and find another place of refuge. They even tried to convince them to continue home with them to Sussex. The brothers politely refused and told the family that even though they knew that being with the resistance meant a life of conflict, they were determined to take their country back. That meant staying in Montreal for them. The siblings had stayed in Montreal for a day to give Ezra some time to heal and then they left the city under the cover of night.

The siblings traveled for the next few days in the darkness of night. They would find what ever shelter they could during the day, as not to be seen by the drones while they rested. The sky had been a constant buzz from the drones when they were in Montreal but the further East they traveled there seemed to be less traffic in the sky. The siblings still wanted to play it safe though. The last thing they wanted was to lead the government back to their home and put their parents in danger.

Although there was an absence of drones in the sky, the family did notice more planes flying overhead. The planes were not the kind of plane that would do surveillance but rather the kind of plane that would carry passengers. The siblings wondered together what this might mean and why so many passengers would be flying toward the Capital.

It was a cold fall morning when the siblings finally reached the town. They stood on what used to be an old highway that overlooked their home. They had longed to see this town again and waisted no time heading straight for the old school. As they began to make their way through the town they walked by familiar surroundings. There was something comforting about this place. After all the fighting and after all the chaos it was nice to finally reach a place of peace and quiet.

They walked the abandoned streets so quickly that they were almost at a run. They continued toward their home until they reached the grown field that separated them from the school. The door of the school opened and out stepped their mom.

"Mom!"

The siblings all yelled at the same time and began to sprint across the field.

Heidi and Drew had gotten up and did what they did their some old morning routine. Drew would wake up, groan, and roll to the side of the bed. Heidi would rub his back and then give him a little shove off the side. Once on their feet they would make sure the animals were fed, the plants were watered, then they would sit down for a little breakfast. Without the kids around their life had become quite quiet.

The couple had gone back to their old home, that they lived in before the Gathering, and picked up some devotions to go through together. This was part of their routine after eating breakfast. Once they had finished devotions they would pray. They spent most of their time praying for the safety of their children. It had been weeks since they had seen the kids and they had become quite worried.

"Well dear. I'm going to head down to the stream and get some water. I won't be long. I love ya!" Drew smiled as he gave Heidi a peck on the cheek.

As Drew turned to leave Heidi returned a smile. She found it harder to smile as the days passed. How could she have let her boys go? How could she have let her daughter be taken? These thoughts constantly haunted her. She knew that if she stayed inside while Drew was gone that she would be left with her thoughts. That was going to make for a miserable day.

Heidi headed for the door and swung it open. The moment the door opened she could see four figures standing at the edge of the field. She wondered if the group were more weary travelers and if they had some news about what was happening in the Capital. The thought barely escaped her mind when she heard her children yell.

Her eyes welled up and her knees began to tremble. She tried to yell for Drew but her voice wouldn't allow it. She took one step toward them, then two, then she was at a full sprint and the gap between the family seemed to vanish in a moment. They met half way across the field and fell into each other's arms. They laughed and cried, and embraced for what seemed like forever.

"Heidi?" The sound of Drew's voice broke through the sound of crying and laughing.

"Dad!!!" The siblings jumped to their feet and bolted across the remaining field toward their father.

Drew was almost to the water when he heard a sound from the school. He didn't know what the sound was so he turned and began to sprint toward the school. He could see a commotion in the field but didn't see Heidi. Had the government returned? He was rounding the corner of the school when he could see Ezra's head peak above the tall grass. The sight stopped him in his tracks. His eyes began to well up with tears and he could hardly see the children or the field in front of him.

Drew was so happy to see Ezra that he hardly heard the sound of the other kids yelling for him. He ran overjoyed straight toward them until the family collided with a thud. They fell to the ground and held each other tight. Nothing was going to be able to separate them. The family was finally back together.

The siblings began to tell their parents about the events that had taken place. They told them about the battles, the chases, and about meeting Auston and Mitchell. They told them all about the Capital and the resistance. They told them about the fights and the victories. The stories went on for ever and got more intense every time they told them. The family had finally reunited and the feeling was better then they even dreamed. The family knew that the government was not going to give up until they tracked them down, but for now, they would enjoy their time together. God had protected them and showed them the value of a loving family. There was nothing in the world more desirable, nothing in the world more important, and nothing in the world more precious than family.

# Epilogue

The family had been reunited for a few days and it was like everything had returned to normal. Almost normal that is. Azalia had taken a keen interest in the training time that the family did daily. She was putting in extra time and trying to make up for all the times she tried to get out of it before. She knew that if the boys could learn to fight then she could learn as well. Azalia was pretty certain that it was not going to be the last time that they had a run-in with the government, but next time, she was going to be ready.

She had trained for hours and it was time to get some sleep. She made her way down the hallway to her room and set her Bible and a glass of water beside her bed. Azalia had been having nightmares since the siblings returned from the Capital. She decided that when she woke up in the night she would grab her Bible, read a few verses, and take a drink. This would usually help her fall back to sleep most nights.

Azalia kneeled down beside her bed and prayed. She had begun to pray and thank God for family and protection, but this night her nightly prayers began to switch focus. God had granted Azalia's brothers the ability to protect the family and even the nation. She began to pray that God would grant her this ability as well. Day after day she would train, but nothing. Night after night she would pray, but nothing. This night seemed no different as she prayed and fell fast to sleep.

She was only sleeping for a couple hours when the dreams started. She could see the Capital and the gates were repaired. The airport was abuzz and planes were traveling in and out constantly. She found herself on the runway and a plane had just arrived. The plane was large and beautiful decorated with the symbol of the Earth painted on the side.

The door opened and a set of stairs were rolled next to it. Out of the plane a woman emerged. This woman must have had authority because no one on the ground would look her in the eye as she made her way down the stairs and across the runway. Azalia knew that this lady was someone to fear.

"Lady Sora."

Azalia knew the voice the moment he spoke, and she recognized his face as he stepped from the shadows. It was Treadon, with his plastic smile. Seeing him again sent a shiver up her spine and left the taste of vomit in her mouth.

"We have been awaiting your arrival. Shall we get to it? I know who they are. I have found where they live and we should be able to end their miserable existence within the week."

Treadon suddenly looked straight at Azalia like she was really standing there and this wasn't a dream. He lifted his hand slowly with a smile still plastered across his face. He pointed his finger straight at her with his hand in the form of a gun. He mimicked pulling the trigger and that's when Azalia awoke from her dream.

Azalia awoke so suddenly that she hit her bedside table and knocked the glass into the air. She felt the glass the moment her hand made contact and as she turn to grab it she caught it mid air. Only her hand wasn't touching it. There she laid in her bed staring at this glass hovering a few feet away from her. This was impossible. She imagined herself placing the glass delicately on the table. As she moved her hand in the direction of her bedside table the glass slowly moved and settled down softly. She had been given the gift that she had desired so badly. If her dream was any indication of the future she was going to need it.

Drew Mallery is available for interviews and personal appearances. For more information or requests email the publisher at: info@advbooks.com


To purchase additional copies of this book, visit our bookstore website at: www.advbookstore.com